AGENT NINE
SOLVES HIS FIRST CASE

*

Agent Nine
Solves
His First Case

By

GRAHAM M. DEAN

A Story of the Daring Exploits
of the "G" Men

WILDSIDE PRESS

CONTENTS

Contents

AGENT NINE
SOLVES HIS FIRST CASE

Chapter I

A SURPRISE CALL

★

Bob houston, youthful clerk in the archives division of the War Department, drew his topcoat closer about him and shivered as he stepped out of the shelter of the apartment house entrance and faced the chill fall rain.

Going back to the office after a full day bent over a desk was no fun, but a job was a job, and Bob was thankful for even the small place he filled in the great machine of government.

The raw, beating rain swept into his face as he strode down the avenue. A cruising taxicab, hoping for a passenger, pulled along the curb, but Bob waved the vehicle away. Just then he had no extra funds to invest in taxi fare.

The avenue was deserted and Bob doubted if there would be many at work in the huge building where the archives division was sheltered.

At the end of a fifteen-minute walk Bob turned

in at the entrance of a hulking gray structure. The night guard nodded as he recognized Bob and the clerk stepped through the doorway.

Bob paused in the warmth of the lobby and shook the water from his coat and hat. Fortunately he had worn rubbers so his feet were dry and he felt there was little chance of his catching cold.

The door behind him opened and a blast of raw air swirled into the lobby.

Bob turned quickly; then hurried to greet the newcomer.

"Hello Uncle Merritt," he cried. "I didn't expect to run into you down here tonight."

Merritt Hughes, one of the crack agents of the Department of Justice, smiled as he shook the rain from his hat.

"I was driving home when I caught a glimpse of you coming in here. Working tonight?"

"I've got at least two hours of work ahead of me," replied Bob.

"Anyone else going to be with you?" inquired his uncle.

"No, I'm alone."

"Good. I want to talk with you where there

is no chance that we may be overheard."

Bob was tempted to ask what it was all about, but he knew that in good time his uncle would tell him.

They stepped into an automatic elevator and Bob pressed the control button.

There was a distinct resemblance between uncle and nephew. Merritt Hughes looked as though he might be Bob's older brother. He was well built, about five feet eight inches tall, and usually tipped the scales at 160 pounds, but there was no fat on his well conditioned body. His hair was a dull brown, but the keenness of his eyes made up for whatever coloring was lacking in his hair.

Bob was taller than his uncle and would outweigh him ten pounds. His hair was light and his pleasant blue eyes were alert to everything that was going on. Both had rather large and definite noses, and Bob often chided his uncle on that family trait.

The elevator stopped at the top floor and they stepped out. Another guard stopped them and Bob was forced to present his identification card. The small golden badge which his uncle displayed was   sufficient   to   gain   his   admittance.

Bob's desk was in one wing of the archives division and they made their way there without loss of time. Bob took his uncle's topcoat and hung it beside his own. When he turned back to his desk, his uncle was seated on the other side, leaning back comfortably in a swivel chair.

"Still have the idea you'd like to join the bureau of investigation of the department of justice?" asked Merritt Hughes. The question was casual, almost offhand, and Bob wasn't sure that he had heard correctly.

"You're kidding me now," he grinned. "You know I'd like to get in the service, but I haven't a chance. Why, I'm not through with my college work, and they're only taking graduates now."

"I'm not kidding, Bob; I'm serious. I think there may be a chance for you to get in. Of course you'd have to finish your college work after you were in the department, but that wouldn't be too much of a handicap."

"I'll say it wouldn't," exulted Bob. "Now tell me what it's all about. The last time I talked to you about getting in, you gave me about as much encouragement as though I was suggesting a swim across the Atlantic ocean."

Merritt Hughes was a long time in answering, and when he finally spoke his voice was so low that anyone ten feet away would have been unable to hear his words.

"There's trouble and big trouble brewing right in this department," he said. "We don't know just exactly what is going to happen, but we must be prepared for any emergency."

Bob started to speak, but his uncle waved the words aside and went on.

"We could plant an agent here, but that might be too obvious. What we need is someone on the inside whom we can trust fully."

Bob, teetering on the edge of his chair, breathlessly waited for the next words.

"I'm counting on you to be the key in the intrigue that's going on right now in this building," said Merritt Hughes. "What about it?"

"You know you can rely on me," said Bob. "Why, I'd do almost anything, take almost any risk to get into the bureau of investigation of the Department of Justice."

"I know you would, Bob, but that isn't going

to be necessary. All I want is someone who will keep his eyes open, listen to everything that is said around here, and report to me each night in detail. You know I wouldn't want you butting into something where you might get hurt."

"But I'm young and husky. I can take care of myself," protested Bob, his eyes reflecting his eagerness.

"Sure, I know you can, but after all I've got to look out for you. Your mother would never forgive me if any actual harm came to you while you were doing a little sleuthing for me."

There was a tender note in the voice of the agent, for it had devolved upon him to watch over Bob and his mother after the death of his sister's husband some six years before. He had been faithful to the trust and he had no intention now of placing Bob in any situation where there would be real jeopardy to his life.

"Go on, go on," urged Bob. "Tell me what I'm to watch for and what you suspect."

Instead of answering Merritt Hughes stepped to the door, opened it, made a careful survey of the hall, and then drew his chair closer to Bob.

Chapter II

AN EMPTY ROOM

★

"WHAT do you know about the new radio developments which have been made recently by the War Department?" he asked.

Bob's surprise was reflected in the look which flashed across his face. There had been only the vaguest of rumors that startling radio advancements had been made by War Department engineers. It had been only thin talk in the department. The clerks mentioning it on several occasions when they had been alone.

"I've heard some talk that rather surprising advancements have been made," said Bob, "but there has been nothing definite known. Of course, some of the clerks have been talking about it."

"But no one has any definite information. As far as you know, the plans have not been filed in the vaults," Merritt Hughes was pressing hard for an answer, but Bob could only shake his head.

"This division handles most of the radio data," he said, "but nothing new has been placed in the vaults here for weeks. I'm simply cleaning up routine stuff."

"If new plans and data were filed, you might handle them," persisted his uncle.

"That's quite likely, but I wouldn't know the contents. Everything comes in under seal and with a key number and only the engineers know the key and the contents of the sealed package."

"Still, you might have a hunch when the papers are important?"

"I might. There is always talk in the department. But I would have no way of actually knowing what was going through my hands."

"I was afraid of that," admitted his uncle. "It makes things all the harder. If you only knew when the plans were going through you would be in a position to use every precaution."

"But I don't take any chances now," retorted Bob. "Extreme care is used with every single batch of plans that are sent over by the engineers."

"Oh, I didn't mean that you were careless, Bob," smiled the Department of Justice agent. "I only meant that if you knew when radio secrets were going through you could use additional care and set up extra precautions."

"You must be afraid something is going to be stolen."

"That's exactly what is troubling me," confessed his uncle, "and I'm afraid that unknowingly you may be involved. I don't want you to get caught in a trap if I can help it. That's why I stopped here tonight. I wanted to have this talk with you, to warn you that there have been important discoveries by the engineers and that they may be through in a few days. From now on watch every single document that is sent through your hands. Don't let it out of your sight from the moment it is delivered to you until you have filed it and placed it properly in the vaults. Understand?"

Bob, his face grave, nodded. "I'll see that nothing like that happens. But who could be after these new plans?"

Merritt Hughes shrugged his shoulders.

"Bob, if I could answer that question this problem would be comparatively simple. The answer may be right here in this department; again it may be some outside force that we can only guess at."

"Are you working alone on this case?" Bob continued.

A shadow of a frown passed over Merritt Hughes' face.

"I wish I were; I'd feel more sure of my ground."

"That means Condon Adams is also on the job," put in Bob, for he knew of the sharp feeling between his uncle and Adams, another ace operative of the bureau of investigation. They had been together on several cases and at every opportunity Adams had tried to obtain all of the credit for the successful outcome of their efforts. He was both unpleasant and ruthless, but he had a faculty of getting results, and Bob knew that for this reason alone he was able to retain his position.

The fact that Condon Adams was on the case placed a different light on it for Bob, for Adams had a nephew, Tully Ross, who was in the archives division of the department with Bob.

There was nothing in common between the two young men. Tully was short of stature, with a thick chest and short, powerful arms. His eyebrows were dark and heavy, set close above his rather small eyes, and his whole face reflected an innate cruelty that Bob knew must exist. If Condon Adams was also on the case, it meant that Tully Ross would be doing his best to help his uncle for like Bob, Tully was intent upon getting into the bureau of investigation.

Bob's lips snapped into a thin, firm line. All right, if that was the way it was to be, he'd see that Tully had a good fight.

Merritt Hughes smiled a little grimly.

"Thinking about Tully Ross?" he asked.

Bob nodded.

"Then you know what we're up against. It's two against two and if you and I win I'm sure that I can get you into the bureau. If we don't, then Tully may go up. What do you say?"

"I say that we're going to win," replied Bob, and there was stern determination in his words.

"That's the way to feel. Keep up that kind of spirit and you'll get in the bureau before you know it. In the meantime, don't let any tricks get away from you in this routine. Watch every document that comes into your hands and let me know at the slightest unusual happening in this division."

"I'll even put eyes in the back of my head," grinned Bob as his uncle stood up and donned his topcoat.

"How long will you work tonight?" asked Merritt Hughes as he opened the door which gave access to the hallway.

"Probably two hours; maybe even three."

"Watch yourself. Goodnight."

Then he was gone and Bob was alone in the high-vaulted room where the rays from the light on his desk failed to penetrate into the deep shadows and a strange feeling of premonition crept over him. For a moment he felt that someone was watching him and to dispell this feeling he turned on the glaring top lights.

The room was empty!

CHAPTER III

BOB HAS A VISITOR

★

Bob turned off the top lights and returned to
his desk, which was one of half a dozen
in the long and rather narrow room at
one corner of the building.

As he sat down he could hear the beat of the
rain against the window and looking out could
see, through the curtain of water, the dimmed
lights of the sprawling city. On a clear night the
view was awe-inspiring, but on this night his
only thought was to complete his work and to
return to the warmth and comfort of his own
room.

Bob delved into the pile of papers which had
accumulated in the wire basket on his desk.
They must be filed and the proper notations
made. There was nothing of especial importance,
or he would not have been working alone for it
was a rule of the division that when documents

of great importance were to be filed, at least two clerks and usually the chief of the division must be on hand. Sometimes even armed guards came in while the filing was taking place for some of the secrets in the great vaults across the corridor were worth millions to unscrupulous men and to other powers.

But until tonight, until his uncle's words had . aroused him, Bob had felt his own work was rather commonplace. There was nothing in his life which compared with the excitement and the almost daily daring of the men in the bureau of investigation of the Department of Justice.

The hours were rather long, the work was routine and his companions, though pleasant, were satisfied with their own careers. They were not looking ahead and dreaming of the day when they might wear one of the little badges which identified a Department of Justice agent.

Then Bob realized that he must stop his day dreaming. Or was it day dreaming after all? His uncle had said that there was now a possibility that he might join the department. But this was no time to ponder about that. He could think of his future when he returned to his room.

Bob went to a filing case which was along the inside wall of the room and extracted a folder. Taking it back to his desk he started making entries of the papers which were on his desk. He worked slowly but thoroughly, and his handwriting was clear and definite.

Others might be faster than Bob in the filing work in the division, but there were none more accurate and when his work was done the chief of the division always knew that the task was well cared for.

Bob worked for more than an hour, stopping only once or twice to straighten up in his chair, for it was tiring work going back to the desk after a full day of the same type of work.

When the file was complete, he returned it to the case along the wall and sorted the papers which remained on his desk. They belonged in four different files and he drew these from the cases and placed them in a row atop his desk.

The air in the room seemed stuffy and Bob walked to one of the windows and opened it several inches—just enough to let in fresh air, yet not far enough for the sharp wind to blow rain into the room. Far below him a car horn shrieked as an unwary pedestrian tried to beat a stop light.

Bob went back to his desk. Another hour and his work would be done. He picked up his pen and resumed the task.

Bob later recalled that he had heard a clock boom out the hour of nine and it must have been nearly half an hour later when the door which led to the corridor opened quietly and a man stepped inside.

The young clerk, at his desk, was so intent upon his work that he did not sense there was a newcomer in the room until the visitor was almost behind him.

Then Bob swung around with a jerk and recognized Tully Ross. There was a momentary flare of anger in Bob's face.

"Next time you come in, make a little noise," he snapped. "I thought a ghost was creeping up on me."

"I'm not much of a ghost," retorted Tully, taking off his topcoat and shaking it vigorously to get the water off. "I didn't know you would be working tonight."

"Couldn't get through this afternoon," replied Bob, "and so much material has been coming in lately I was afraid that if I let it go another day I'd be swamped."

"Next time that happens let me know and I'll give you a hand," volunteered Tully as he sat down at his own desk, which was two down from Bob.

Bob nearly laughed aloud for the thought of Tully volunteering to help anyone else was almost fantastic. Each clerk had a special type of filing and each was not supposed to exchange work with the other. In this way there was little chance for the others to know what documents were going through for permanent filing.

"Thanks, Tully, that's nice of you," said Bob, "but I don't know what the chief would say."

"He'd never need to know," said Tully swinging around in his chair.

"But if he did find out that we were helping each other, we'd both be out of a job and I can't afford to take that kind of a risk."

"Neither can I right now," conceded Tully, "but I hope to get into something better soon. This doesn't pay enough for a fellow with my brains and ability."

"I'll admit that it doesn't pay a whole lot," replied Bob, "but a fellow has to eat these days."

"Some day I'm going to be over in the Department of Justice," said Tully definitely. "It may not be tomorrow or next week, but I'm going to get there."

"I think you will," agreed Bob. "You've got the determination to keep at it until you do." What he failed to add was that Tully's uncle would do everything in his power to see that Tully got the promotion and it was no secret that Condon Adams had powerful political connections that might be helpful in getting Tully into the bureau of investigation.

Chapter IV

THE DOOR MOVES

★

TULLY was in a talkative mood and at such times he displayed a pleasing personality. This was one of those times, but to Bob it was more than a little irritating for he had work to do and every minute passed in talking with Tully meant additional time at his desk.

"I've had a funny feeling lately that things were tightening up in here," said Tully. "Even tonight this room doesn't feel just right."

"It's the wind and the rain," said Bob, looking up from his work. "When the sun is out tomorrow you'll feel much better."

"I don't know about that. Say, Bob, you haven't heard of anything special breaking? Something may be coming over from the engineers that is unusually important."

Bob couldn't honestly say no, so he made an indefinite answer.

"There's always talk," he said.

"Sure, I know, but this time it's different. I've heard that the radio division has made some startling discoveries that more than one foreign power would give a few millions to have in its possession."

"What, for instance?"

"That's just it," confessed Tully. "There's only vague talk; nothing you can put your finger on."

"I thought they kept that stuff pretty well under cover," said Bob, who was determined to feel out Tully and learn just how much the other clerk knew. It was evident now that Condon Adams had been talking to his nephew, probably telling him in substance much of what Merritt Hughes had divulged to Bob earlier in the evening and now Tully was on a fishing expedition to learn just what Bob knew. Well, two could play that game and Bob, his head bent over his work, smiled to himself.

"Well, they never advertise the papers they're sending over for the permanent files," Tully said, "but you know how things get around in the department. Sometimes we have a pretty good idea what's going through even though it is all under seal and in a special code."

Bob nodded, for Tully was right. In spite of the secrecy which usually surrounded the filing of important documents, the clerks often knew what was going through their hands, for even the walls in Washington seemed to have eyes and ears and whispers flitted from one department to another in a mysterious underground manner which was impossible to stop. Sometimes the conjecture of the clerks was right; again they might all be wrong. But it was on such talk as this that secrets sometimes slipped away and into the hands of men and women for whom they had never been intended.

Bob's division, which filed all of the radio documents, had enjoyed a particularly good record. The chief, Arthur Jacobs, had been in charge since before World War days, and he had used extreme care in the selection of the personnel. There was yet to come the first major leak and Bob hoped fervently that it would not happen while he was in the division.

Tully puttered around his own desk, shoving papers here and there and obviously making an effort to appear interested. Once he glanced sharply at Bob, who was intent on his own work.

Finally Tully stood up and walked to one of the windows. He gazed out for several minutes and Bob, glancing up at him, got the impression that Tully was trying to make up his mind what to do.

The next thing Bob noticed, Tully was on the other side of the room, pulling open one of the filing cases. The floor was carpeted and his steps from the window to the filing cases had been noiseless.

There was no rule against a clerk opening one of the cases, for the documents kept there were of no major importance. Something in Tully's attitude caught Bob's attention. Then he realized that Tully was looking into one of the files which was under Bob's supervision and there was a strict rule against that.

Bob hesitated for a moment. It seemed a little foolish to make an issue over that. Probably Tully had done it absent mindedly. Then he remembered his uncle's warning to watch everything going on in the division.

"Tully, you're in the wrong file," said Bob.

Tully turned around quickly, his face flushing darkly.

"No harm, I guess. I just wondered what you've been doing and how you've been handling your file. I heard Jacobs complimenting you the other day and thought I could get some good pointers by looking your stuff over."

"That's okay, Tully. I'll show you sometime when Jacobs is here, but you know the rule about the files. I'll have to ask you to close that one."

"And suppose I don't?" snapped Tully.

"Oh, you'll close it all right," said Bob. His voice was still calm and even, but there was a note of warning that Tully dared not ignore.

Bob closed the file on his desk and stood up, stretching his long, powerful arms. Tully didn't miss the significance of the motion for Bob had a well founded reputation as a boxer.

Tully turned back to the filing case and slammed the steel drawer shut.

"There you are, Pollyanna," he retorted. "That file doesn't look so good after all."

"Just so it suits Jacobs; that's all that concerns me," said Bob, sitting down again.

Tully picked up his topcoat to leave.

"Well, anyway I don't envy you staying on here alone tonight. This place is giving me the creeps."

After Tully had departed, Bob was able to concentrate fully on his own work. A clock boomed out again, but he was too preoccupied to count the number of strokes. For all he knew it might have been ten o'clock, or perhaps even eleven.

A sharp knock at the door disturbed Bob.

"Who is it?" he demanded.

"Guard. Just checking up. How long are you going to be here?"

It was the first time in many nights of overtime work that a guard had ever checked up, but Bob decided that it might be a new rule placed in effect without his knowledge.

"Half an hour at least," he replied.

Apparently satisfied, the guard moved on and Bob could hear his footsteps growing fainter as he bent to his task again.

But he was not to work long uninterruptedly. The telephone buzzed and there was obvious irritation in his voice when he answered. But it vanished when he recognized his uncle's voice.

"I was a little worried," explained Merritt Hughes, "when I phoned your room and found you weren't in. Everything all right?"

"Yes, except I've had too many interruptions," said Bob. Then he hastened to explain. "I don't mean you though. Tully Ross was in and sat around for nearly an hour without doing anything except making me nervous."

"Did he hint at anything?" asked Bob's uncle.

"Yes. The same thing you mentioned. Evidently Condon Adams has told him about it. You know Tully wants a position in the bureau of investigation, too."

"Sure, every youngster in the country would like it," replied Merritt Hughes. "Better stop for tonight and run along home and get some sleep. I want you on the alert every hour of the day. You're in the office from now on."

"I'll be through in less than half an hour," promised Bob. "Then I'll go directly home."

"It's a bad night and getting worse. Take a taxi and don't run the risk of catching cold."

This Bob promised to do and with a sigh hung up the telephone receiver and bent once more to the task of finishing the filing.

As the hours of the night advanced, the wind grew colder and Bob arose and closed the window. The air in the room was now damp and it would have been easy to allow his mind to run riot for the building was strangely silent. Noises from the street, far below, were smothered in the sound of the rain, driven against the windows.

A slight creak startled Bob and he whirled toward the door. Even in the dim light which his desk light cast he could see the handle of the door moving. Fascinated, he watched. The handle was moving slowly, as though every effort was being made to guard against any possible noise. Bob remained motionless in his chair as though he had suddenly turned to stone.

Chapter V

A SLIVER OF STEEL

★

THE time seemed endless. Actually it could only have been seconds that Bob sat there watching the turning of the doorknob. Then the knob started back. Unseen fingers had learned what they wanted to know. The door was not locked.

Through the hulking building there seemed no sound except Bob's own strained breathing. In the corridor it was as quiet as in the room, yet someone must be outside the door, testing the lock.

Bob shook his head. He must be dreaming. His nerves must be over-wrought from too much work and on edge from the talk he had earlier in the evening with his uncle.

Reaching out, he tilted the shade of his desk lamp back and a flood of light struck the door-knob. No! His eyes had not tricked him. The knob was still turning. There was a faint click and then the knob remained stationary.

Bob leaped into action. In one fast lunge he was across the room, his hands gripping the door-knob. He tugged hard, but the door refused to open. Then he paused for hurried footsteps were going down the hall. Bob shouted lustily. Perhaps his cry would reach the guard at the elevators.

Then he shook the door. It couldn't be locked, of that he felt sure. Bracing himself again he tugged at the door and almost fell over backwards when it suddenly opened.

Bob stepped into the corridor. There was no one in sight but from a distance he could hear someone hurrying toward him. A guard came around a turn in the corridor.

"Did you call just then?" demanded the watchman.

"I'll say I did," replied Bob. "Someone was trying the door here and when I tried to open it, the door stuck. Then I let out a whoop. Didn't you see anyone?"

"No one came my way," said the guard quickly, but his eyes did not meet Bob's squarely.

"We'd better look along this end of the corridor. If someone was here, he might have slipped into one of the other offices."

Bob shook his head.

"No, he wouldn't have done that. Besides, I distinctly remember hearing him running down toward the elevators."

"Well, I wasn't asleep and no one came my way," insisted the guard. "Maybe you were dreaming a little. You look kind of tired."

"I am tired, but this was no dream," insisted Bob. Then he remembered the door. What had made it stick? It hadn't been locked.

"Give me your flashlight," said Bob and the guard handed over a shiny, metal tube.

Bob turned the beam of light on the floor, and searched closely.

"What are you looking for?" asked the guard.

"For the reason why the door stuck," said Bob tartly. Then he found it—a thin sliver of steel that had been inserted as a wedge. It was an innocent enough looking piece, but when placed properly in a door could cause considerable delay.

Bob picked it up and placed it in his pocket.

Although he was not aware of it at the time, it was the first piece of evidence in a mystery which was to pull him deep into its folds and require weeks of patient effort to untangle.

The guard had edged over to the door and now reached out to pull it shut. Only a sharp order from Bob stopped him.

"Keep your hands off the doorknob," he ordered. "Someone was tampering here and I don't want you messing your hands around the place."

The guard hesitated as though undecided whether to obey Bob, and the clerk stood up and doubled up a fist.

"Better not touch that door." There was a steelly quietness in the words that decided the guard, and he stepped well back into the corridor.

"You'd better get back to your post. I'll take care of this situation," said Bob. "I'll keep your flashlight and return it to you when I leave the building. I want to do a little scouting around and may need this light."

The guard grumbled something under his breath, but retreated down the corridor and

finally vanished from sight. Bob disliked him
thoroughly for his attitude had been one of sullen defiance; so unusual from the men generally
on duty at night. It might be well to speak to
Jacobs about it in the morning.

Just to make sure that no one came along and
touched the doorknob, Bob took out his handkerchief and tied it around the knob in a manner
which would protect possible fingerprints.

That done, he picked up the flashlight again
and started to reconnoiter in the corridor, trying
one door after another. There was just a possibility that the marauder had found a hiding place
in an office which had been left unlocked. Bob
knew that it was almost a useless quest, for the
offices were checked each night.

He made the rounds along one side of the corridor and started back on the side opposite his
own office. The night lights were on and at the
far end of the corridor it was necessary for him
to use the flashlight.

Door after door proved unyielding to his
touch and he was about to give up the quest when
he came upon a door that swung inward when
his hands gripped the knob.

Bob drew back suddenly and flashed the beam of light into the long room, which was almost identical with the one in which he had been working. What he saw there startled him more than he dared to admit later, and he stepped inside and moved toward the nearest desk.

The ray from the flashlight revealed the utter confusion in the room. Baskets of papers on top of the desks had been upset and even the drawers in the filing cabinets had been pulled out and their contents hurled indiscriminately over the floor.

A slight sound startled Bob and he swung around, the beam of light focusing on the door.

It was closing—swiftly and silently.

Bob leaped forward, stumbled over a wastepaper basket, and then reached the door which clicked shut just before he could grasp the handle.

Bob tugged hard on the door, but like the one which led to his own office, it stuck.

Could it be another wedge of steel? Bob wondered and braced himself for another lusty tug. The door gave way and Bob toppled backward in a heap, the flashlight falling and blinking out.

Bob had fallen heavily and for a moment he remained motionless on the floor listening for the sound of someone moving along the corridor. He could have shouted for the guard, but an inward distrust of the man kept him from doing that. Instead, he groped around for the flashlight, turned it on, and got to his feet, considerably shaken in mind and body by the experiences of the last few minutes.

The young clerk reached for the light switch and a glare of light flooded the room, revealing even further the destruction which had been wrought there.

Bob looked around. Hundreds of papers had been strewn on the floor; some of them had been ruthlessly destroyed and he wondered how many valuable documents would be lost when they finally checked up.

But this was no time for inaction, he decided, and he hastened to one of the desks and picked up a telephone. He dialed quickly, but it was nearly a minute before a sleepy voice answered.

"Hello, Uncle Merritt?" asked Bob anxiously.

"No, I'm not home; I'm still at the building. I wish you'd get down here as soon as you can.

"No, I haven't had an accident, but some mighty strange things have been going on around this floor tonight. One of the offices has been completely ransacked. I'm in it now. Papers have been thrown all over and the filing cases opened and a lot of stuff destroyed.

"Who did it? Gosh, I wish I knew. Someone's been shutting doors on me and leaving steel wedges in them. It's giving me the creeps."

"I'll be right down," promised the Department of Justice agent.

Bob placed the receiver back on its hook and backed out of the room. The fewer things he touched the better it would be and as he drew the door shut, he was careful to keep his hands off the knob for there was a possibility of valuable fingerprints being there.

An eerie feeling raced up and down Bob's spine as he turned toward the door which opened into the office where he worked. The building was so quiet it was disturbing, yet he knew some unknown maurauder had been busy on the floor while he had been bent over his desk. Could the unknown be after the radio secrets his uncle had hinted about? It was certainly worth considering.

Bob reached the door that led into the office where he worked and stopped suddenly. He felt cold all over as he stared at the doorknob. He remembered distinctly having wrapped his own handkerchief around the knob to preserve possible fingerprints. But there was no handkerchief there now and the door was slightly ajar. The light had been on when he stepped into the hall, but now the room was in inky darkness.

CHAPTER VI

IN THE DARKENED ROOM

★

Bob paused on the threshold of the long office, staring into the blackness of the room. After his recent experiences he couldn't be blamed for hesitating a moment.

Should he close the door, back into the hall and await his uncle's arrival or should he snap on the lights and see what had taken place in the room? It seemed to Bob that he pondered those questions for several minutes; actually it was less than five seconds.

He reached for the light switch at the left of the doorway and pushed the button. But there was no answering blaze of light; only the dead click of the switch.

Bob knew then that the lights had been tampered with, that more than likely someone was lurking in the shadowy darkness of the office. His better judgment told him to wait until he could summon assistance, but some other urge drove him on. He couldn't explain it later; he simply went ahead.

The young filing clerk stepped across the threshold, the flashlight in his hand aimed down the center of the room. Then he turned on the flash and a beam of light cut through the darkness.

Bob gasped. The light showed papers strewn over the floor and the drawers from desks and filing cases pulled indiscriminately out and dumped on the floor.

The shock of the confusion in the office brought him up short. Then he started to swing the light about the room to determine the full extent of the damage by the marauder.

A slight noise to the right caught Bob's attention and he turned in that direction. Instinctively he knew that danger lurked there, and he tensed his body. It came before he was ready; something hurtling out of the dark; something that struck his right hand a numbing blow; something that sent the flashlight crashing to the floor where the lens and the bulb shattered and the light went out.

But the blow sent Bob into action. He must get back to the door and get it closed; that would cut off the one avenue of escape for the intruder.

The clerk leaped backward, his hands reaching out for the doorway. He collided with someone else; someone wearing a topcoat still damp from the rain outside.

Bob thought quickly. He must find some way to stop the other if for only an instant. He drew back his right foot and swift kick connected with the unknown's shins with such force that an involuntary cry rang through the room. Bob leaped on and crashed into the half opened door. With anxious fingers he found the key on the inside, slammed the door shut and turned the lock.

That done Bob dropped down on the floor where he would have a chance to rest, to collect his wits, and to plan his future course of action.

For a time there was no sound in the room. He could not even catch the breathing of the other man and he thought of the possibility that the other had slipped out the door before he had closed it. Then he dismissed that as an impossibility for there had not been sufficient time for that.

Bob knew every inch of the long office; knew where every desk and chair was located and every window. As his eyes became more accustomed to the dark he could pick out the lighter blots which were the windows.

Then a slight noise caught his attention. The unknown was moving, probably on his hands and knees, feeling his way toward the door. Bob couldn't resist a chuckle as he thought of the dismay that would spread through the other when he found the door securely locked and the key missing.

Just to be on the safe side, Bob edged away from the door and sought shelter behind a nearby desk. To make sure that he would move noiselessly he slipped off his shoes and placed them beside a filing cabinet where he wouldn't fall over them if it was necessary for him to make a sudden move.

Strangely enough Bob felt very calm. His heart beat rapidly and his breath came shorter and faster, but his mind was remarkably clear, his hands steady. He was glad now that he did not have the flashlight, for using it would only have made him a target for the marauder.

Bob wondered how long it would take his uncle to reach the scene. Probably another ten minutes, for Merritt Hughes lived a considerable distance from the building. What might happen inside that room in the next ten minutes was something that Bob didn't care to guess about.

As Bob listened he could hear the almost noiseless movements of the other man and knew that he was nearing the door. Then he heard hands moving along the woodwork—finally the gentle turning of the doorknob. Then there was the sharp rattle of the knob as though a sudden wave of anger had swept over the man at the realization that he had been trapped in the room.

Bob moved away from the door, crawling on his hands and knees, and he kept going until he was well down the room and right at the steel cabinet where the radio documents were filed. With cautious hands he felt along the front of the case. So far the drawers had not been pulled out for they were identified only by key numbers instead of by the name of the type of papers which they contained.

This was one cabinet Bob was determined to protect, for, after what his uncle had told him earlier in the night, he felt sure that this was the object of the unknown's visit.

Once more the doorknob was rattled sharply; then silence again shrouded the room and Bob felt his nerves tightening. It was tough waiting alone in the darkness. He wondered if the other man possessed a gun and if he would have the nerve to use it if an emergency caught him.

Bob strained his ears for some sound of the other's maneuvers. A faint sort of "plop" made him smile. It sounded very much like a shoe being placed gently on the floor. Several seconds later there was a similar sound and Bob knew that they were now on even terms; neither one of them having his shoes on. This man was no fool; he was determined to keep his own movements as secret as possible.

Then Bob heard a sound which was anything but heartening. The unknown was coming toward him. He could hear the gentle scrape of knees as the man crawled along the floor. He was evidently feeling his way along the filing cabinets and Bob moved out toward the center of the room where he found protection between two desks, set fairly close together.

His action was not a minute too soon, for he had barely settled himself in his new position when he saw a darker shadow moving along in front of the filing cases. The man was less than six feet away, and breathing very quietly, but steadily.

Bob held his own breath as the man passed along the row of filing cases. Evidently he was going to make the rounds of the room in an effort to catch Bob by surprise, overpower him, and take away the key. Bob chuckled inwardly at that thought. He was too familiar with the room to be caught in that manner.

Moving out slightly from behind the shelter of the desks, he saw the man reach a window and raise his head so that he could look down on the street. It was a temptation that Bob couldn't resist and he picked up an inkwell on the desk beside him, took careful aim, and hurled the heavy glass container.

Just as he threw the inkwell, Bob slipped and the noise attracted the attention of the other man. He leaped to his feet and whirled about. The glass container, instead of striking the man's head, hit his shoulder, glanced into the window and crashed its way on out into the darkness.

There was a cry of pain from the intruder and then a sharp burst of flame as a bullet scarred the top of the desk which shielded Bob.

Bob went cold all over. There was no more fun in this thing. It was deadly serious now and he knew that his very life might depend on the events of the coming minutes for this man was cornered and capable of shooting his way out if necessary.

CHAPTER VII

SIRENS IN THE NIGHT

★

As the echoes of the shot died in the room, Bob realized that he had been foolish in throwing the inkwell. It had unduly alarmed the other man and placed his own life in jeopardy. The slug from the gun had come much closer than Bob wanted it to.

There was only one consolation. The shot should attract the attention of the guards on duty in the building and within a minute they should be at the door, battering their way in. Against superior numbers Bob felt that the intruder would not put up a resistance with gun play.

Bob stared at the windows. The head and shoulders of the unknown had disappeared and the distant noises of the street were clearer now, drifting in through the broken window.

Merritt Hughes should arrive at almost any minute and Bob felt that the wise and sensible thing now was to play as safe as possible and await the arrival of help.

Crouched down between the desks, he was in a position to watch the file with the radio documents and he knew that if they were molested he would fight with all his strength to protect them.

As the seconds passed into minutes Bob felt his muscles tensing and his nerves becoming tighter.

There was no sound in the room; there had been no sound since the echoes of the shot had died away. Had his missile disabled the other man; had the shot been fired involuntarily? They were questions he couldn't answer.

Why didn't a night guard appear in the corridor outside? Bob believed that he would have risked a call for help if anyone passed. But strain as he might, he could hear no one outside the door.

Then Bob broke into a cold sweat. The man who had fired the shot was almost beside him.

Bob had been so intent upon listening for some sound in the corridor that he had failed to hear the unknown crawling toward his own hiding place.

Bob sensed, rather than saw, what was happening. He could hear the steady breathing of the other and he held his own breath. Would the man crawl on down the room toward the doorway or would he turn in between the desks where Bob had sought shelter?

The dark blob that was the other's head and shoulders appeared between the desks and Bob waited for an agonizing interval. Then the figure moved on and Bob could breathe once more.

That had been a close call.

Then came another sound that brought Bob back to the alert. There was the faint shrilling of a siren.

Was it a fire alarm? Bob listened intently. No, it was sharper, more penetrating. A police car. That was it!

It was evident that the other man had also heard the night alarm for Bob heard a muffled exclamation. He doubted if it was an alarm turned in by his uncle for his protection, but at least it was enough to alarm the marauder and Bob's muscles snapped back to steelly tension. He had gone so far now that he had no intention of allowing the other to escape at the last minute.

. The steady wail of the siren drew nearer as down on the avenue the speeding machine dashed through traffic lights and skidded past other machines which were pulling over to give it the right of way.

The siren rose to a crescendo and then died to a wail as the police car swayed to a stop somewhere below and Bob knew then that rescue was near. His uncle, feeling the need for quick re-enforcements, had evidently called on the Washington police and commandeered a cruising radio car.

From somewhere out of the darkness came a low, deadly voice.

"Listen, kid, this spot is getting tough. Give me the key to this door or I'm going to turn this gun loose and it will be just too bad if I get you. I've got plenty of extra clips and I'm going out of here on my feet. Give me that key!"

Bob knew there was no time to lose for there was a ring of panic in the other's voice and you never could tell what a panic-stricken man would do.

The desks afforded little protection from a barrage of bullets and Bob quickly edged his way out from behind them and in between two steel filing cases. While these were not intended to be bullet proof, at least they were much better than oak desks.

"Did you hear me?" called the voice from near the doorway. "Give me that key."

Bob slipped his hands into his pockets, and pulled out a key ring. The key to his own room was somewhat similar to the one that fitted the door of this office. He quickly detached this and tossed it toward the door.

He couldn't afford to cry out now for he knew the man near the door would shoot. The key fell on the floor and he could hear the frantic efforts of the other to locate it. Then came a gasp of relief from the unknown and Bob heard him fumbling at the keyhole, trying to insert the key and turn it in the lock.

There was a sharp cry from the man at the door.

"You've tricked me. Give me the right key. Give it to me!" The voice was nearing a hysterical pitch and Bob smiled grimly.

The man couldn't stand the dark and the certain knowledge that outside men were speeding toward that very room, men who would shoot first and ask questions afterward.

Bob wondered whether tossing another key would again trick the man at the door.

Before he could decide there was a stab of flame in the blackness and a bullet crashed through the desks where he had been hiding.

"Come on; give me that key!" The voice was hysterical now, a scream that cut through the room and echoed out the shattered window.

Down below another police siren was ebbing as a second car pulled up at the curb and disgorged its load of armed men, who rushed into the building to follow the lead of the first detail.

Bob faintly heard elevator doors clang open. It would be only seconds now until they were at the door, beating their way in.

By this time Bob's eyes were well accustomed to the darkness and he could distinguish the shadow of the man crouched near the door, listening now to the pounding of the police as they charged up the long corridor.

"Bob, Bob! Where are you?"

It was Merritt Hughes and Bob thrilled at the voice of his uncle. Then dismay filled him for he knew what would happen if they broke down the door and charged into the room for a trapped man is always dangerous.

Fists beat against the door and two ribbons of flame streaked from the gun, the bullets crashing through the door and out into the corridor.

Bob couldn't help shouting a warning.

"Keep away; he's desperate!"

The answer to that was another shot into the desks where he had been hiding and Bob knew that the man felt sure he was still hiding there.

There was a sudden silence in the corridor and Bob knew that his uncle and the police were conferring on the best way to break into the room. As he listened he saw the man near the door moving, backing down into the room where Bob was hiding and if he kept on coming he would pass within a foot or less of Bob.

Bob felt his muscles tightening and he breathed deeply. If he could only disable the unknown, it would solve what promised to become a highly dangerous situation.

The man was coming noiselessly, in his stocking feet, his head cocked toward the door where he listened for some further move.

A yard, two feet and now only inches separated them. Bob was ready. His hands shot out and caught the other man in a steelly grasp that choked an involuntary cry from him. At the same time Bob kicked with all of his strength. The blow caught the other man behind the knees and Bob could feel him crumpling.

The gun, which he had feared the most, clattered to the floor and they were on equal terms, ready now to fight hand to hand.

As they fell the other man twisted about and Bob knew that his adversary was no weakling. He could feel the muscles of the other man's arms tightening and a short, sickening blow that started at the floor caught him on the chin.

Bob was weak all over for a moment, an interval just long enough to give the other a chance to collect his wits. Then Bob was at him again, his arms held in close, his fists raining blows like a trip hammer. They were hard, fierce jabs that would have rocked an ordinary man to sleep in less than ten seconds. He heard the other gasp as a right caught him in the midrift, but he came back for more.

Fighting in the dark was dangerous business.

A wild blow might send his hand crashing into a steel case or against a desk and his knuckles might be broken but it was a chance Bob had to take and he slammed away with a will.

Suddenly the man went limp. Bob caught him, fearing a ruse, and shot home one more hard right. Then he knew that the other was out—out cold, and he suddenly went weak himself.

Fists were beating against the door.

"Open up, open up!" It was Merritt Hughes' voice.

Bob managed a reply.

"Coming," he called. "Just a minute."

"You all right?" demanded the federal agent, but Bob was too weak and tired to reply.

Somehow he managed to dig the key out of his pocket and with trembling fingers he found the keyhole, inserted the key and turned the lock. The door burst open to reveal Bob standing on wavering legs, and Merritt Hughes caught him just as he collapsed.

CHAPTER VIII

THE PAPER VANISHES

★

LIGHTS from a whole battery of flashlights seemed to blaze down at Bob and he blinked hard as Merritt Hughes leaned over him.

"Bob, Bob, are you hurt?" demanded the ace federal agent.

Bob managed to shake his head. Just then he was too exhausted even to talk.

As he watched the flashlights swept around the room, revealing its wild disorder. Then the lights focused on the form of a man sprawled out under the nearest desk and Bob caught his breath for the man was in a uniform of one of the night watchmen. So that was the reason why there had been no response to his calls for help; the marauder had been the guard!

Merritt Hughes stepped over to the unconscious form and gazed at the man's face.

"You certainly landed a haymaker on one eye," he told Bob. "Know who he is?" Bob managed to sit up where he could glimpse the other man.

"He's the guard who was on duty tonight," he said, "but I don't know his name. He is a new man."

Merritt Hughes chuckled grimly.

"Well, he's going to a lot different place. Maybe he'll be able to remember his name and tell us a few things when he wakes up. Now just what happened here?"

"It's a long story," began Bob.

"Then save it until we're alone later. Was anyone else running around up here tonight except yourself and the guard?"

Bob thought instantly of Tully Ross, then decided to wait and tell his uncle about that when they were alone.

"This fellow was the only intruder," replied Bob, which was true enough, for Tully belonged to the office staff.

"Take him down to the nearest station and have him fingerprinted and photographed," the federal agent told the policemen.

The officers leaned down and picked up the man Bob had fought and managed somehow to get him to his feet. Supporting him on their shoulders they walked him down the hall and Bob heard the elevator doors click.

Bob's uncle tried to turn on the lights in the room, but the switches, though they snapped as usual, failed to send any current into the lights.

"Fuses blown," Bob heard him mutter.

They were alone now, the police having departed with their prisoner.

"Here's an extra flashlight, Bob. See if you can find anything missing by making a hurried search around the room," directed Merritt Hughes.

Bob felt stronger now and he got to his feet. He was still a little unsteady, but the cool, rain washed air, coming in sharp gusts through the window now, cleared his head and he took the flashlight which his uncle offered.

The twin beams of light swept around the room.

"What a mess!" exclaimed the federal agent, as the lights revealed the utter confusion.

"Who's in charge?" he asked.

"Arthur Jacobs is the filing chief for this room," replied Bob.

"Then you'd better get him on the telephone and see that he gets down here at once. Explain what's happened and tell him that you want to check over the files for any possible missing papers."

Bob looked up the number of the filing chief's home telephone and dialed. It was some time before a sleepy voice answered and when Bob informed the filing chief who was speaking the voice was sharp and angry.

But when he imparted the news and added that a federal agent was waiting for his arrival and the checkup, the filing chief promised to come down at once.

In the meantime a janitor came up from somewhere below and fixed the fuses so that there was ample light in the long room.

"I can start in checking up on the files now," said Bob, but his uncle held out his hand.

"I don't want a thing touched until the filing chief is here," he explained. "Then, if something important is missing, you'll have a clean bill of health."

"But I'm sure that nothing important has come through lately," said Bob. "Of course we don't know definitely when important records are being filed, but we usually have a pretty good hunch."

"Then here's hoping that your hunch has been right," replied his uncle.

Bob told him about the condition of the other room down the hall and they went there and examined it at some length, finally deciding to lock and seal the door until morning when a more thorough inspection could be made.

By the time they were back in the room where Bob worked, the elevator doors clanged open and they could hear impatient footsteps hurrying toward them.

Arthur Jacobs, short, heavy and round-faced, fairly popped through the door. His blue eyes went wide as he saw the litter of papers in the room and Bob felt sorry for the filing chief for Jacobs had a splendid record of efficiency.

"What under the sun happened?" demanded Jacobs. "I'm afraid I was so sleepy I was sharp with you over the phone," he told Bob.

"I guess I would have been a little provoked at

being routed out at this time of night," admitted Bob. "I guess my uncle can tell you better than I can."

Arthur Jacobs, after glancing again at the wild confusion of papers on the floor, faced the federal agent.

Merritt Hughes described the events of the night briefly and Bob saw the filing chief casting anxious glances toward one of the steel cabinets. His own heart missed a beat or two for the cabinet that appeared to be worrying the filing chief was the one in which the newest radio documents were kept. It was here that any papers relating to new discoveries in this field would be placed.

But Bob managed to reassure himself. He was convinced that only the man he had caught could have been in the room and there had been no way for him to get rid of any papers which he might have stolen from the file.

Then Arthur Jacobs interrupted the federal agent.

"Just a minute. Some important papers came through late this afternoon and I placed them in one of the files myself. I want to be sure that they're here."

The filing chief stepped to the radio filing cabinet and skimmed through the papers with expert fingers.

Bob saw the frown of anxiety deepen on the filing chief's face as his fingers sorted the documents expertly. Jacobs shook his head and then bent down and scanned each document on the floor in front of the case.

"Anything important missing?" asked Merritt Hughes.

Jacobs didn't answer at once, and when he finally looked up, Bob read the answer in his face.

"Yes," said the filing chief in a voice so low that it carried only a few feet, "the papers which came over this afternoon have vanished."

Chapter IX

SUSPICIONS

★

Bob and his uncle stared at Arthur Jacobs with unbelieving eyes, and the filing chief saw their doubt.

"The papers are gone—gone I tell you." His voice rose almost to a frenzy for this was the first time that such a thing had occurred in his usually well ordered and carefully routined department, and he had visions of losing his job.

"Yes, yes, we heard you," replied Merritt Hughes. "But perhaps you missed them in going through the file. Let's go through together."

"It won't do any good," said Jacobs in a flat and hopeless voice. "I know this file from A to Z and the papers that came in this afternoon are not here."

The federal agent paused and looked hard at the filing chief.

"You say they were important papers?"

Jacobs nodded. "They were so important that I refused to trust them to anyone else."

"You're sure no one in the department knew these papers were coming through?" insisted the federal agent.

"I can't be sure," replied the filing chief, "for there has been talk drifting around the last few days about some important radio discoveries that have been made by the army engineers. But I am sure that no one knew the exact time these papers came over."

"Was it a complete file on the new discoveries?" asked Merritt Hughes anxiously.

"I don't know, but from the usual procedure, I would say that it was only a partial file. Just as a precautionary step they usually send the records of new formulas, and developments over in several sections so that it would be almost impossible to take one section and know what it was all about."

"But you're not sure about this special file?"

"No, except that it was small; a single sheet of paper in a sturdy manilla envelope."

"We'd better go through everything in the room," decided Bob's uncle, and they got down on their hands and knees and started rummaging through the litter of papers.

It would take days to place these back in their proper sequences and Bob felt sorry for Jacobs.

They finished one side of the room and started down another. There was no sign of the missing envelope and Bob's uncle phoned the precinct police station to learn if such an envelope had been found on the prisoner.

"Search him again," he instructed the police when they informed him that no envelope or papers of any description had been found.

Bob looked toward the half opened window.

"Do you think it would have been possible for him to toss that paper out the window and have it picked up by someone on the ground?" he asked.

Merritt Hughes went to the window and looked down. It was better than a hundred feet to the ground and the sharpness of the wind had not lessened. He shook his head.

"I don't think that happened," he said. "It would have been too risky. Either that paper is still in this room or it was taken out by that fellow when he left."

"But the police haven't found anything," protested Bob.

"Sometimes even the police slip up when they run into an especially clever crook and this man had to be clever to get in here in a guard's uniform and stand night duty."

Their search of the room neared an end and Arthur Jacobs looked even more downcast.

"I knew it was missing when I failed to find it in the file," he groaned. "This is where I lose my reputation."

"Don't worry about that. We've got to find this paper first," said Merritt Hughes. "Go through the file once more."

With the federal agent on one side and Bob on the other, the filing chief examined every paper in the cabinet, but without success.

Merritt Hughes turned on his nephew.

"You're sure that you were the only one in this office until this fellow got in?" he asked Bob.

Bob hesitated, wondering whether he dared implicate Tully Ross by mentioning his name. But Tully had been there and the disappearance of the radio document was too important to let anything like that interfere, he decided.

"Well, Tully Ross dropped in for a few minutes," said Bob.

"Why didn't you tell me this in the first place?" asked the federal agent, and Bob felt the color in his cheeks mounting at the rebuke which was implied by his uncle's words.

Chapter X

ON THE LEDGE

★

ARTHUR JACOBS wheeled around sharply, at the exchange between uncle and nephew.

"What was Ross doing here at night?" demanded the filing chief.

"I guess he just dropped in; saw the lights burning up here and wondered what was going on," replied Bob.

"Did he touch anything, work on anything?" There was a desperate note of anxiety in the filing chief's voice and Bob knew that Jacobs was thinking only of the reputation of his department rather than linking Tully to the events of the night.

"No, he only offered to help me, but I told him I was getting along all right," said Bob.

"Did he ask you about any of the papers you were filing?" pressed the federal agent.

"Well, not exactly, but he did mention something about the radio secrets. That's been more or less common knowledge in the department that something big was breaking and we have all been curious about it."

"Did Tully touch this file or go into it?" demanded the filing chief.

Bob hesitated. Tully had looked into the file, but he hadn't removed anything Bob was sure.

"Well, did he touch anything?" pressed Jacobs.

"He did open this file," admitted Bob, "but I looked up just then and I am sure that he didn't remove anything. In fact, I don't think he touched anything inside the file."

"Why did he open the file?" asked Merritt Hughes.

"Well, he mentioned something about wanting to see the way I kept my files. I guess he said he had heard Mr. Jacobs say he liked the way I handled them."

Jacobs smiled for it was no secret with him that Bob was his star assistant, while Tully was probably the poorest of the clerks who worked in the filing room.

"You're sure Tully didn't take anything out?" insisted his uncle.

"I can't be positive," said Bob, "but I don't believe anything was removed by him."

Merritt Hughes was silent for a minute. When he spoke again he addressed his words to Bob.

"Get Tully on the telephone and tell him to dress and get down here right away."

From the tone of his voice, Bob knew that it would be useless to say anything more in defense of the other clerk and he went to the telephone and dialed Tully's apartment number. It was two o'clock now and an unearthly hour to rout anyone out of bed, so Bob prepared himself for a long wait at the telephone. He was not disappointed for it was at least three minutes before a sleepy voice answered and Bob recognized it as that of Tully.

When he explained that the other clerk must come down at once, there were sleepy protests and Bob's uncle, provoked at Tully's attitude, took the phone.

"Tully, this is Merritt Hughes. There's been trouble in this office tonight. You are one of two outsiders who were in here. If you know what's good for you, get down here at once and don't argue."

With that he hung up the receiver without giving Tully an opportunity to answer.

"I think he'll be down without losing any time," he said, and Bob was ready to agree.

Tully lived some distance from the office. Bob knew that it would be nearly half an hour before he could arrive.

"Let me have a flashlight," he said to his uncle, "and I'll go down on the ground floor and see if there is any chance that paper was thrown from the window."

Merritt Hughes nodded his agreement and handed a light to Bob.

"I'll go along," said Arthur Jacobs. "I can't stay up here and do nothing."

The filing chief was visibly shaken and Bob was glad enough to have companionship for there would be no fun in prowling through the shrubbery at the base of the building at that hour of the night.

They walked down the corridor together and turned and faced the elevator entrance. The cage came up in answer to their summons and they dropped swiftly toward the first floor.

"Find out yet what happened to the regular guard on our floor?" Bob asked the elevator operator.

"They've checked his home, but he left there right on time. It's a cinch he never reached here, though. This building has been searched from top to bottom and there's no sign of him."

When they stepped out on the main floor there was evidence of suppressed activity for several guards, flashlights in their hands, hurried past them.

"They're even searching the closets," volunteered the elevator operator, "for the fellow who was caught up on your floor was wearing the guard's uniform."

Bob whistled softly. This was getting more serious every minute. He wondered about phoning the news upstairs to his uncle. But he decided against that. They would soon return to the upper floor and he could tell him then.

The night was as blustery as ever and Bob drew his topcoat close as the first gust of wind and rain swept down on them. The flashlights threw feeble glows ahead of them as they floundered through the shrubbery which flanked the base of the building.

"Ouch!" cried the filing chief as a piece of shrubbery snapped into his face and Bob turned to help him.

"Go on; I'm all right," said Jacobs and they pushed ahead, Bob in the lead.

Back and forth they beat their way through the shrubbery, their lights held close to the ground. Time after time they stopped to pick up a sheet of paper in the faint hope that it might be the missing radio document they were seeking so anxiously.

Now they were directly under the windows of the office. Bob, looking up, could see the glow of lights from the windows. Here they were doubly careful to make a thorough search and Arthur Jacobs went over every inch of the ground with his own light, stooping to be sure that no scrap of paper went unobserved.

The quest looked hopeless and Bob stood up to ease his aching back.

"Guess we might as well give up," he said. "Tully will be here in a few minutes and we'll want to be back upstairs when he arrives."

"There's just a chance the paper might have been blown around the corner," said the filing chief, who was determined to cling to even the most slender hope.

"Well, there's a chance, but it's a mighty slim one. We'll have a try, though," agreed Bob.

The rain was even sharper as they turned to the corner of the building and the lights attempted to pierce the blackness of the hour.

For five minutes they crawled back and forth underneath the shrubbery. Bob was chilled now and a trickle of water, coming off his hat and dropping down his neck, did nothing to improve his spirits. His knees and back ached and it would seem good to get back into the office where it was light and warm and there would be no rain to face.

"I guess we've looked under every shrub on this side of the building," finally said Arthur Jacobs and there was a bitter note of disappointment in his voice. "We might as well give up and go back."

Bob straightened up and the beam from his flashlight struck one of the deep, recessed windows that were on the ground floor. The ledge in front of the window itself was at least two feet wide and it was on this ledge that the beam of light centered.

Bob cried out involuntarily and Arthur Jacobs, hearing the cry, whirled to his side.

Something was on that ledge; something that was shrouded in black. Bob's heart leaped with an emotion that was one of combined fear and curiosity and with Jacobs at his side he plunged forward through the shrubbery.

Chapter XI

STRAINED TEMPERS

★

Bob was the first to reach the ledge, which was about two feet above the ground level and well protected from the onslaughts of the storm.

His flashlight revealed the figure of a man, swathed in a dark blanket, jammed up against the window.

Bob was reaching for the blanket when Arthur Jacobs seized his arm.

"Don't. We'd better wait until we can get your uncle down here."

"No," decided Bob, "we'll find out what this is all about right now."

With that he pulled the blanket off the figure and stared down into the pain-wracked eyes of the guard who was usually on duty on his floor. A gag, which had been ruthlessly put in place, made speech for the captive out of the question.

"Run for help!" Bob told Arthur Jacobs and the filing chief departed as rapidly as his short legs would carry him.

While he was waiting for help, Bob busied himself in an effort to unfasten the captive's bonds.

Picture wire had been used to bind the man's hands and wrists and the gag was of rough, heavy material which was held in place by strips of adhesive tape. It was to this that Bob gave his first attention for from the expression in the guard's eyes he knew that the gag was causing him untold agony.

With capable but gentle fingers, Bob worked at the gag until the cruel bandage was freed. He bent down close to hear the first whisper from the man's lips.

"Water, please!"

Bob half propped the captive up and then turned in quest of some water. Anything halfway decent would do. Nearby a small torrent was coming from one of the drain spouts. It had been raining for hours, so the spouting should have been clean.

The filing clerk cupped his hands under the

spout and got a double handful of water. This he carried back to the ledge and let it trickle into the other's mouth.

He was just finishing his task when Arthur Jacobs, followed by half a dozen guards, appeared on the run, the beams from their flashlights cutting a broad swath of light through the darkness.

` The guards picked up the captive and carried him inside. Blankets were produced, the wire was cut from his hands and feet. By this time Merritt Hughes, who had been notified, was down on the ground floor. He took charge immediately.

"Get this man to a hospital at once," he directed. "Two of you go along to see that he talks with no one. Understand, no one. I'll be around soon and talk with him as soon as they get him into bed and take every precaution to avoid pneumonia."

Bob felt sorry for the guard. He had been stripped of his uniform, bound and gagged and had been helpless on the ledge for hours. It would be a miracle is he did not suffer an attack of pneumonia.

An ambulance, which had been summoned, arrived, and they saw the guard lifted into the vehicle. Two other guards climbed in beside him.

"Remember, no one is to talk with him until I arrive," Merritt Hughes ordered.

As they turned to re-enter the building, the federal agent spoke to Bob.

"Tully Ross got here just before the guard was found. Come along upstairs while I question him."

They were waiting for the elevator when a short, thick-set man hastened in. He was scowling and obviously had been routed out of bed.

Merritt Hughes turned to greet the newcomer and as he recognized him there was no cordiality in the greeting.

"Hello, Adams," he said. "I didn't expect to see you here tonight."

"I'll bet you didn't," snapped the other, "but don't think for a minute you can bull-doze my nephew and get away with it."

"What do you mean?"

"You know darned well what I mean. Didn't you just phone Tully Ross and order him down here; didn't you practically threaten him?"

"I wouldn't call it exactly a threat, but I did tell him to get down here at once if he knew what was good for him. No clerk is going to be impudent with me."

Merritt Hughes spoke firmly and calmly, but there was something in the flash of his eyes that told Condon Adams that he had gone far enough.

"If you want to come along while I talk with Tully, you're quite welcome," he added.

Condon Adams grunted and shouldered his way ahead of them and into the elevator.

They were silent as they rode up to the top floor and strode down the corridor to the office where Tully Ross was waiting for them.

Tully's dark, rather handsome face, was marked by frowns as he saw Bob enter behind Merritt Hughes.

"Now what's been going on here?" demanded Condon Adams as he surveyed the room with cool, calculating eyes. Suddenly he saw the radio file and he swung to face Merritt Hughes.

"This case getting hot?" He shot the question out in short, chopped-off words.

Bob's uncle nodded.

"Looks like it."

"Fine one you are not to let me know," said Adams bitterly.

"I don't recall that you've ever tipped me off to any breaks in any case we've worked on before," said Merritt Hughes coolly. "When you get in that habit I'll try to learn your telephone number."

Condon Adams snorted.

"About what I expected. Well, let's get along here. What happened?"

"You'll learn all that in good time," said Bob's uncle. "Right now I'm in charge and I want to know why Tully came up to the office tonight and why he tried to look through the radio file. Speak up, Tully."

"There isn't much to tell," began Tully. "I was going by and when I saw the lights on in the office I came up. Just curiosity, I guess."

"Sure it wasn't anything more?"

"Sure."

"Then why did you try to look into the radio file?"

Tully shot a bitter glance at Bob for he realized that Bob was the only source of information on his activities while he was in the room.

"That was curiosity, too. You know there's been talk around about some important papers coming over."

Arthur Jacobs wrung his hands.

"Talk, talk, talk. Are there no secrets any more in this department?"

"Not many," retorted Tully, who appeared to take malicious glee in taunting the filing chief.

"That's enough, Tully. You know there have been serious happenings. Bob was attacked by a marauder who had gone through the files here."

"What was he doing out of the room; how did anyone get in?" It was Condon Adams' turn to speak.

Bob replied sharply, explaining what had happened.

"I'd call it mighty poor judgment on your part to leave this room no matter what the circumstances," said Adams. "I think I'll lodge a complaint against you."

"That's going far enough," Merritt Hughes said firmly. "You'll do nothing of the kind. If this thing is going to get as personal as that I'll file one against your nephew for coming up here and attempting to get into a file that is prohibited to him. Now how would you like that?"

It was obvious that Adams did not relish the suggestion and the whole matter of filing complaints was dropped right there.

Merritt Hughes took charge then, questioning Tully carefully about all of his actions while he was in the room. Tully was surly, but he answered truthfully enough.

"How about it, Bob?" asked the federal agent.

"What's the matter? Doubt my word?" flared Tully, his dark face flushing.

"Simply checking," said Bob's uncle and the tone of his voice invited no further remarks from Tully.

"Tully's told exactly what happened up until the time he left the room," said Bob.

"Then suppose you tell us what happened after he left and you were left here alone," interjected Condon Adams. There was an unpleasant inflection in his voice that Bob resented; an implication that Bob might have been responsible for whatever had taken place that night. Merritt Hughes got it, too, but he ignored it.

Bob told his story in a straight-forward manner. Once or twice Adams interrupted to ask questions, but he gained little satisfaction from his efforts to heckle Bob.

"Well we've got two more sources of information," said Merritt Hughes. "One is the man who was captured in this room and the other is the guard who was found on the ledge down below."

"Which one are you going to question first?" asked Adams.

"I don't know. It's late now. I think I'll see them in the morning."

"Not trying to give me the slip, are you?" the words shot out of Adams' mouth, which was twisted into a bitter sneer.

"I'm simply handling this case in my own way," replied Merritt Hughes evenly.

"Oh, I don't know whether it's your case or not. Remember that both of us have been assigned to this radio angle. Well, you do the work and I'll get the information out of your reports. It will save me a lot of tedious detail. Come on, Tully."

Condon Adams, moving as rapidly as his short, thick legs would carry him, left the room and Tully, with a backward glance of mingled relief and unsatisfied curiosity, trailed after him.

Merritt Hughes, watching them depart, shook his head and Bob heard his uncle mutter, "What a precious pair."

"What are we going to do now?" asked Bob.

"We're going home and get some sleep. You've been through enough for one night. Jacobs, see that he is relieved of routine tomorrow. I want him with me when I question these men."

"I'll make the necessary arrangements," promised the filing chief, who was still looking disconsolately at the mess of papers scattered over the floor. "Use Bob as long as you need him and I'll fix up the reports here. Good luck and good night."

"Good night," replied the federal agent and Bob echoed the words. They strode down the hall together, entered the elevator, and when they reached the entrance of the building were fortunate enough to hail an owl cab which went cruising by.

The air was fresh, but the rain, coming down steadily, was driven by a sharp wind and the night was as raw as ever.

CHAPTER XII

STEPS IN THE HALL

★

BOB leaned back in the taxi. It was restful
listening to the steady hum of the tires on
the wet pavement. His uncle looked at
him quizzically.

"Pretty much all in?" he asked.

Bob nodded. "Well, I'm willing to admit that
I'm more than a little tired and my muscles ache
a good bit from that tussle in the dark back in the
office. I thought for a minute that fellow was
going to get away from me. It's a good thing you
put in an appearance when you did."

"I knew speed was essential and I corralled a
few of the local police to help me out," chuckled
Merritt Hughes. "Still think you'd like to be a
real federal agent?"

"And how!" said Bob sincerely. "It's got the
thrilling kind of a life I'd like to follow."

"Don't make the mistake of thinking it is all

thrills and fun. There are months upon months when the cases are the merest of routines and the work is real drudgery. But every so often something bobs up that does add a zest to living. Where do you suppose that radio document went?"

"I wish I knew. Jacobs will worry himself sick until it is recovered. I knew something was in the air, but none of us thought anything important had been sent over."

"Well, someone knew it and that someone must have had inside knowledge. There was no guess work in rifling those files."

"No, but someone got into the wrong office the first time," said Bob, recalling the ransacking of the other office on the same corridor. He felt in his pocket for the thin steel wedges which had been used in the doors. Snapping on the dome light in the taxi, he held them in the palm of his hand.

"These wedges were used in an attempt to lock the doors and keep me in," he explained. "I forgot all about them until just now. What do you make of them?"

His uncle looked at them sharply, but refused

to touch them. Pulling out a clean handkerchief, he had Bob drop the wedges into the cloth, covered them carefully and placed them in an inside pocket.

"I'll turn them over to the laboratory. They may be able to find some fingerprints if they haven't been handled by too many people."

"I'm the only one who's handled them outside of the man who put them in place," declared Bob, who felt that here might be a really important clue.

The taxi swung toward the curb. A dull light gleamed over the entrance of the apartment house where Bob had a room.

"Sure you're all right?" his uncle asked.

"Absolutely. I'll take a shower and hop into bed. Don't forget to stop for me when you go down town to interview those fellows."

"That's a promise," agreed the federal agent.

Bob jumped out of the cab, hurried across the parking and into the entrance of the apartment. Turning, he watched the cab pull away from the curb. Then he inserted his key in the lock and entered the building. The air was warm and dank and it made him sleepy.

His room was on the third floor at the back and the lights in the hallway were none too bright. Bob's room was part of an apartment occupied by an elderly couple, but it had an outside entrance on the hallway and he could come and go as he pleased.

Another feature of it was a private bathroom. In spite of its comparative luxury, he was able to obtain the room for a rent well within his modest means for Bob also acted as a sort of caretaker for the apartment when the older people were away on one of their extensive trips.

Bob unlocked the door of his room. He had left one window partially open and the air here was fresh. Turning on the lights he undressed quickly and stepped into the bathroom where he was soon under a shower.

A rough toweling down made his body glow and then he pulled on fresh pajamas. The clock on the dresser showed the time to be three thirty. The night was nearly gone when Bob tumbled into bed and turned off the light on the bedside stand. In less than a minute he was sound asleep.

Bob's slumber for the first hour was deep and dreamless. Then his mind, as his body threw off part of the fatigue, became restless and pictures of the events of the night flashed through his brain. Bob stirred restlessly once or twice and finally aroused enough to mutter in his sleep.

He must have been reliving the vivid struggle in the darkness of the office for he was tense when he sat up suddenly—wide awake and listening for some sound from the hall.

Sleep vanished from his eyes. There was no mistake about it. Someone was outside his door, trying the knob ever so gently. At that moment Bob longed for some other weapon than his two capable hands. The side of the bed nearest the door creaked and Bob knew if he eased his body over that edge the creaking of the bed might scare away the marauder. Moving cautiously, he slid out the side next to the wall and put his bare feet on the floor.

An alleyway ran back of the apartment and a street light at the head of this sent just enough light down to mark the window as a lighter square against the general pattern of darkness.

This turning of the door knob was getting to be too much for Bob and he cast about for some object which he could use as a club. His golf bag was in the corner and he managed to extract a steel shafted midiron which would make an excellent weapon if he had a chance to swing it.

There was no thought of fear in Bob's mind as he moved toward the door. His bare feet padded softly across the floor and he reached out and touched the doorknob with his finger tips. It was moving.

For a moment Bob recoiled like he had been struck by an electric shock. Then he got a grip on his nerves and reached down for the key which he had left in the lock on the inside of the door.

To his surprise the key was not in the lock. Then he understood the slight noise that had aroused him. Whoever was on the other side of the door had pushed the key out of the lock and the noise made when it had struck the floor had brought him out of his sleep.

Bob leaned down and felt along the floor. He reached out in his search for the key, became overbalanced, and before he could regain his equilibrium, dropped to his knees with a thud that was plainly audible in the hall.

Bob's hands closed on the key he sought, but

as he drew himself upright again he heard someone running down the hall. Seconds later came
the slam of an outside door and Bob knew that it
would be useless to attempt any pursuit.

He turned on the light and opened the door.
The same dim lights were burning in the hallway.
Closing the door, he was sure that it was locked
and then wedged a chair under the doorknob.

When Bob got back into bed he was a sadly
perplexed young filing clerk. Why should an
attempt be made to enter his room? The riddle
was beyond him. Perhaps his uncle could solve
it in the morning.

Chapter XIII

BOB FIGHTS BACK

★

Bob's nerves were tight. The mystery of the turning knob had aroused and sharpened his senses and sleep was slow in coming to him again. He tossed fitfully on the bed, turning the pillow several times in an effort to find a more comfortable place for his head. When he finally dropped asleep it was just before dawn.

Once asleep, Bob fell into a heavy slumber that was finally broken by the strident ringing of the telephone at the stand beside his bed. It was with an effort that he sat up in bed and reached sleepily for the instrument.

"Hello," he said in a voice still drugged with sleep.

Then all thoughts of sleep were swept from his mind by the message which came over the telephone. It was from his uncle.

"The head of the bureau of investigation wants

you to come down for an interview at eleven o'clock," said Merritt Hughes. "Think you can make it?"

"What time is it now?" asked Bob.

"Nine-thirty."

"I'll be there with half an hour to spare," promised Bob. "I've got a lot to tell you."

"Anything happen?" There was a note of anxiety in the question.

"Not quite. Tell you about it later. Where will I meet you?"

The federal agent named an office in the Department of Justice building and Bob promised to be there right after breakfast.

He hung up the receiver and piled out of bed. His muscles were still a little sore as a result of the encounter of the night before, but a snappy shower toned up his body and when he finished dressing he felt that he was ready for anything the day might have in store in the way of excitement and adventure.

Bob put on his topcoat and then removed the chair which he had wedged under the doorknob. In the cool light of the morning, the events of the night before seemed fantastic yet he knew that one man was in jail while another was in a hospital.

Bob stepped into the hall and carefully locked the door. More or less as a reaction he looked cautiously up and down the hall and then laughed at himself. It was just a plain hall and his fears seemed so ridiculous now.

It was 9:45 o'clock when Bob stepped out of the apartment building. He paused a moment to turn down the brim of his hat for the glare of the sun was too bright for unprotected eyes.

Across the street a large, dark sedan was parked and several men were apparently waiting for someone to emerge from the apartment house opposite. Bob turned and strode down the street. There was ample time for him to have a leisurely breakfast and still reach the Department of Justice building with plenty of time to spare.

The young filing clerk stopped at a nearby restaurant where he usually had breakfast and ordered rolls and coffee. Several morning papers were on the table and he scanned them with unusual interest.

Washington reporters were unusually alert and it was just possible that they might have received some hint of what had taken place last night. Bob went through every page, but there was no story even remotely connected with the night before.

He put down the papers and turned to his breakfast, wondering what the chief of the bureau of investigation wanted. Of course it must be linked with the radio document, but Bob felt that his uncle could adequately give all of the information needed.

Then another thought flashed through his head. But it seemed ridiculous. Yet his uncle had mentioned only the night before that there was a possibility. Bob's great ambition was to become an agent of the Department of Justice and in that ambition Tully Ross was a bitter rival.

Bob finished his breakfast and started walking toward the Department of Justice building. The air was bracing and he swung along at a good pace, unaware of a sedan which was following at a discreet distance.

The filing clerk turned a corner and started down a little used street which was a short-cut toward his destination. As he turned, the car following him spurted forward and closed in the distance. Bob was less than fifty feet down the block when the car swung around the corner. The squeal of the tires as the wheels were cramped caught Bob's attention and he turned around to look at the sedan.

He recognized the machine instantly. It was the car which had been parked across the street from his own apartment house. Something in the intentness of the driver and the alertness of the man beside him sent a wave of apprehension pounding through Bob's veins. He felt sure that the car was on that street for no good purpose and he was the only pedestrian in sight.

Bob knew the short street thoroughly. Beside him was a rather high iron fence that protected a private home. Just inside the fence was a clump of barberry so thick they were almost a jungle of shrubbery. There was no protection across the street and it was a good two hundred feet to the intersection where he could hope to obtain help.

Bob heard the car slow down now and he steeled himself for what he felt was going to be an unpleasant encounter. Just why he had that premonition he could never tell, but in later days, his hunches were to serve him well.

The driver of the sedan had a scar on his forehead while the passenger in the front seat, who was nearest Bob, had red hair that frizzled out from beneath a soft felt hat.

The car stopped at the curb and the passenger jumped out, leaving the door open.

"Say, buddy, I'm looking for an address near here. Maybe you can help me."

"Sorry, I'm afraid not. I'm in a hurry," retorted Bob, edging a little closer to the iron picket fence.

"Oh, I guess you're not in such a hurry. Matter of fact, I've got a little business with you. Ain't you a filing clerk down in the archives division of the War Department?"

"Maybe I am and then maybe I'm not." Bob's reply was crisp.

"Smart guy, huh? Well, I know who you are and I've got business with you."

Bob measured the other, wondering just how hard he would have to hit him to knock him out. The red head was about five feet eight tall, but was compact.

"We're going to take a little ride and talk. See?" There was a threat in every word.

"I'm not riding this morning," he said firmly.

"Give him a crack on the noodle and drag him in," called the man at the wheel of the sedan. He started to get out of the car and Bob knew that between the two of them they would be able to overpower him.

"You asked for it," he muttered as his right swung in a short, hard chop that landed on the red-head's solar plexus. The blow caught the other man napping and doubled him up. Bob was ready for him and a hard cross with his left to the chin ended all thoughts of a fight which might have been in the other's head.

"Hey, you," yelled the driver. "You can't get away with that."

Bob saw him reaching for his back pocket and tugging at something. That decided Bob, who felt sure the other was reaching for a gun. Putting his hands on the fence, Bob vaulted the iron barrier.

He landed in the tangle of barberry, but the shrubbery was so tall that he crashed through and a protecting thicket shielded him from the eyes of the man on the other side of the fence.

Without waiting to see what was happening

in the street, Bob beat his way through the shrubbery. The thorns tore at his clothes and his hands
were soon streaked with scratches, but his
thought was to get as far away as possible in the
shortest time.

CHAPTER XIV

SPECIAL AGENT NINE

★

As Bob clawed his way through the dense shrubbery there was a sharp explosion behind him. Whether it was a shot or the exhaust of the sedan was something he didn't stop to find out.

When he was finally clear of the barberry, Bob found himself in a small, open yard in front of the house, which was heavily shuttered and evidently unoccupied. But Bob wasted no time in reconnoitering the house. He kept on going, running around to the rear.

The iron fence enclosed the whole property but there was a gate and he made for this. A heavy padlock secured the gate, but Bob scrambled over without tearing his clothes and dropped into the alley.

From far behind on the other street he could hear the heavy roar of an exhaust and he ducked into a half opened garage on the other side of the alley for he had no intention of being caught out in the open.

When the noise of the exhaust finally died away, Bob went back into the alley. A walk of a block and a half brought him to a thoroughfare and he hailed a passing cab, directing that he be taken to the Department of Justice building.

Once inside the cab, Bob sat back to take stock of the damage which the thorns of the barberry had done to his hands. There were half a dozen raw angry scratches and innumerable little snags in his suit from the prickly stuff.

When he thought of what had happened in the last few minutes, Bob frankly admitted that he was at a loss to account for it. Why should he be singled out for an attack by a couple of hoodlums? Why should someone attempt to enter his room in the night? Perhaps his uncle would have the key to answers when he met him.

The cab pulled up in front of the Department of Justice building and Bob paid the driver and stepped out. Several pedestrians going by looked at him curiously and he realized that he looked strangely unkempt.

Bob stepped inside the building. His hands were smarting and he took out two clean handkerchiefs and wrapped them around his hands. There was still a little time before his appointment and he turned around and went to a nearby drug store where he explained that his hands had been scratched by barberry. A clerk recommended an antiseptic solution and Bob washed his hands thoroughly in this and then wrapped the handkerchiefs around them again.

Back in the Department of Justice building, Bob was whisked to an upper floor and a boy guided him to the room he inquired for. There was no name on the glass panel of the doorway and Bob stepped inside, wondering just what kind of a reception he was going to have. There was no one in the room when he entered and he sat down in a chair near a window to wait.

The door opened again and Tully Ross stepped in and stared at Bob. The surprise was mutual.

"I didn't expect to find you here," exclaimed Tully, and there was no pleasure in his words.

"Guess that goes for me, too," replied Bob.

Tully took a chair a few feet from Bob and

conversation ended right then and there. For at least ten minutes no word was spoken until an inner door opened and Merritt Hughes entered.

"Hello, Bob. Hello, Tully. You're right on time. Mr. Edgar will be here in a few minutes."

Bob had seen Waldo Edgar, chief of the bureau of investigation of the department of justice several times, but he had never been introduced to him. Through the exploits of the bureau in recent months in tracking down some of the nation's most notorious criminals, Edgar had become an almost legendary figure for it was from his office far up in the Department of Justice building, that he directed, by telephone, telegraph and radio, the great man hunts for the violators of the law.

Merritt Hughes looked at Bob's hands.

"Hurt your hands in the fight last night?" he asked.

"Nothing like that," replied Bob. "I got tangled up in a barberry hedge a few minutes ago and the thorns almost got the better of me. Guess I've ruined this suit."

"What under the sun were you doing in a barberry hedge?" the federal agent wanted to know.

"Trying to get away from a couple of plug-uglies who seemed to want my company more than I wanted theirs."

"No!" exclaimed his uncle incredulously.

"Yes!" retorted Bob with equal insistence. "I was taking a short cut when a sedan pulled alongside me and one fellow got out and asked about an address. It was just a stall to get near me, but I had seen the car parked earlier just opposite the apartment. I was suspicious and when I thought he got insistent I let him have a couple. The driver started after me and when I thought he was reaching for a gun I went over the fence and dove through the barberry."

Merritt Hughes whistled softly.

"This is serious. Have you reported it yet to the police?"

"No. I thought it was best to come right here and tell you. I didn't get the number of the car for I was too busy trying to crash through that blamed barberry."

"That's not important. They've either abandoned the car or changed the license plates by this time. Can you describe the men who were in it?"

Bob supplied a detailed explanation and his

uncle jotted the facts down on a small card.
"This will give us a lead to work on. Later
we'll go over to the bureau of identification and
run through some pictures of red heads and men
with scars on their foreheads. Maybe we can
pick up some real clues there."

Bob was tempted to relate the incident of the
early morning at his room when someone had
tried to gain access, but he hesitated to tell this
in front of Tully. It sounded a little like a fairy
tale or the work of an overwrought imagination.

The door to an inner suite of offices opened
and a dapper, well-built man of about 38 stepped
into the room. Behind him was Condon Adams.

Bob felt his pulse quicken for even before their
introduction he recognized Waldo Edgar, ace of
all the federal manhunters and chief of the
bureau of investigation.

Edgar looked at the handkerchiefs on Bob's
hands and smiled quizzically.

"Fighting?"

"No, just plain barberry thorns," replied Bob.

"Then I take it you weren't strolling on the
barberry just for the fun of the thing," said the
federal chief.

"Well, it wasn't exactly a stroll," grinned Bob. "It was something like trying to do a hundred yard dash in nothing flat through half an acre of barberry. It was a good place to hide, but a poor place for running."

Waldo Edgar's eyebrows went up questioningly and he turned to Merritt Hughes.

"Does this tie in with what happened last night?" he asked.

"Apparently. Bob was trailed by a couple of hoodlums in a car. When he was alone on a side street they waylaid him, but he knocked one out and jumped over a fence and ran through a barberry patch to escape. He came here directly after that happened."

"Anything else happened since last night?" The question was from the thin, straight lips of Waldo Edgar and Bob told in detail what had taken place during the early hours of the morning.

"Why didn't you tell me about this, Bob?" exclaimed his uncle.

Bob flushed. "Well, it seemed like I'd been having enough excitement for the last twenty-four hours and this sounded sort of crazy."

"I'll say it sounds crazy," snorted Condon Adams and Bob caught a supercilious sneer flit across the lips of Tully Ross. It was plain that neither Adams nor his nephew believed the story and Bob turned back to the federal chief.

"There's nothing crazy about this story. It only confirms our realization that some tremendously powerful force is after these radio secrets. We know now that only a part of the secret papers were taken from the file last night. The others had not been sent over from the radio engineering division of the War Department."

"But how could those papers get out of the office last night?" put in Condon Adams.

"That's for you and Hughes here to determine. You're on this case, but I'm going to add a couple of special agents to help you out. It isn't that I think you're not capable, but I believe several inside men in the archives division will be tremendously helpful to you and I don't want to have outsiders go in there."

Waldo Edgar turned toward Bob and Tully and looked at them through searching eyes. His scrutiny of Bob was fairly brief, but he appeared to be making a more careful appraisal of Tully, and Bob thought he saw just a flicker of doubt in the federal chief's eyes.

"It is decidedly irregular for this division to take on additional men, and especially very young men, but when we feel a case merits unusual attention, we do not hesitate to cut away the red tape and employ the individuals we want to serve us. Bob, would you consider joining the bureau of investigation as a provisional agent, working directly out of my office and solely upon this radio case?"

Bob's heart went into his throat and he choked in answering.

"I'd like that very much, sir. I'll do my best."

"I feel sure that you will. Tully, how about you?"

"Great stuff. Count me in."

Waldo Edgar nodded.

"I thought you would both agree. Wait just a moment."

The federal chief left the room and when he returned he had a Bible in one hand and several small leather cases in another.

"Place your left hands on the Bible and raise your right hands," he directed. Then he read a brief pledge, which they repeated after him.

The pledge administered, Waldo Edgar handed one of the leather cases to Tully and the other to Bob.

"You will find your identification cards in there as well as a small gold badge. Further instructions will be given you later in the day. I'm expecting a great deal from each of you."

After shaking hands with each of them he hurried away and Bob looked down at the identification card in the leather case. He was now Bob Houston, Special Agent Nine.

Chapter XV

A REAL JOB AHEAD

★

THERE was a strange mist in Bob's eyes as he looked up at his uncle.

"Shake, Bob. You've got a real job ahead of you and I know you'll come through with flying colors."

"Thanks a lot. This is the biggest thing that has ever come to me and I'm going to succeed if it is at all possible."

There was a grim sort of a chuckle from Tully Ross, who had shoved his leather case with its card and badge into an inside pocket.

"You're going to have to step some if you think you can put anything over on me."

Tully and his uncle left the office and Bob watched the door close behind them.

"Nice people," he grinned.

"I don't like the looks of this case," said his uncle. "It isn't pleasant to think that you've got someone else in the same department, who goes out of his way to make it unpleasant for you, working on the same case."

"Then why is Adams assigned to team up with you?" asked Bob.

"Perhaps because we have a habit of getting re-sults," admitted Merritt Hughes, with a rueful smile. "We've been pretty lucky on a number of cases where we have worked together. The breaks have been about fifty-fifty and now we both want a really smashing victory that will bring us advancement. It looks like this may be the case, but it's going to be dangerous business."

"What do you mean by that?"

"Well, look back over the events of the last few hours. We know that an important paper, containing part of a new radio discovery, was sent over to your department from the radio engineering division. Before it can be properly filed, a guard is overpowered and two offices ran-sacked to find this paper. Later in the night another attempt is made to enter your room and this morning there was an attempt to kidnap you. Looks to me like you're in a key position, but I don't know just what it is yet."

"I'll admit the attempt to get into my room last night and the trouble this morning have me worried," said Bob. "I'm only a filing clerk so why such attention should be centered on me is a mystery."

They walked out into the corridor.

"We'll stop at the bureau of identification and see if we can learn anything about the fellows who tried to kidnap you," said the federal agent.

They dropped down a floor and entered a long room where a number of clerks were working at filing cases.

Merritt Hughes walked up to a slender chap busy at a flat-topped desk.

"Look alive, Jimmy," he said. "There's business at hand."

Jimmy Adel, chief of the filing division, looked up.

"Hello, sleuth. Who are you trailing this morning?"

"One red head and one fellow with a scar on his forehead."

"Now isn't that a lot of help! Don't you know that there are a good many red heads and a whole lot of people with scars on their foreheads? Just be a little more exact, please." But he grinned as he chided the federal agent.

"Jimmy, this is my nephew, Bob Houston. He's detailed to help me on a new case that's breaking pretty fast."

"The radio case?"

"You hear about that?"

"Sure, it's all over the department. Looks big to me. Adams working on it too?"

Merritt Hughes nodded.

"That means you'll have to step fast. I hear that whoever solves this thing will be in line for an inspectorship."

"Hope you're right, Jimmy, because Bob and I are going to clear up this mystery. That is, if you'll give us a little help. A couple of hoodlums tried to kidnap Bob a while ago. He can give you an accurate description of them and you may be able to pull their pictures out of the files."

"We'll find them for you if they've any record at all." He pulled a blank form from a file and fired question after question at Bob on height, weight, color of eyes, and any possible peculiarities which they might have had. When he had finished both forms, he leaned back in his chair.

"I'd call that an almost perfect description of these chaps. If we don't dig them out of the files, I'll miss my bet. We'll get something for you before midnight. Good luck."

Bob and his uncle left the identification bureau and took an elevator down to the main floor. Bob's hands still smarted from the scratches they had suffered from the barberry and he kept the handkerchiefs wrapped around them.

"I want to drop in at the police station and question the man caught last night," said Merritt Hughes, "but we can stop at your apartment on our way down and give it the once-over. We might find something of interest in the hall."

The federal agent flagged a taxi and they sped swiftly toward Bob's apartment.

"Well, how does it feel to be a federal agent, even though you're only a provisional one?" his uncle asked.

"I'm not quite used to it," replied Bob, taking out the small leather case and extracting the card and badge which it contained.

He turned the badge over carefully in his fingers. His name was engraved on the back and behind this small emblem stood the mighty law enforcement machinery of Uncle Sam. Bob thrilled even though he was as yet a small and comparatively unimportant part of that great system, which was rapidly building up a world-wide reputation for "getting its man."

Merritt Hughes settled back in the cushions.

"This is likely to be a rather long-drawn out case," he said, "and from the way it's started, it may be extremely dangerous. When it comes to that, I want you to step aside and let the regular agents take the chances. Do you understand, Bob?"

"But I'm not afraid of trouble," insisted Bob.

"That isn't it. When the pinches come we want men who have been tried under fire in there. You'll be used as an inside man in the archives division and in that capacity you are going to be highly important. There must have been a leak somewhere, else how would it have been known that a part of the new radio development had been sent over for filing? It will be up to you to find where this information leaked before Tully Ross and Condon Adams learn it."

The federal agent paused a moment, before continuing.

"After we find the leak in your department, we'll have something to work back on. That should lead us to the man or the men who now have the papers that disappeared last night."

"Won't the man arrested last night be the key to that?" asked Bob.

"Perhaps, but I hardly believe so. Usually the boys who do the rough stuff in a case like this know little of what is really going on. But we'll see him a little later. No use in letting anything slip."

The cab slowed down in front of the apartment house and Bob's uncle paid the taxi bill.

They walked up to the third floor and then back along the corridor to the door which opened into Bob's room. The door was slightly ajar and Merritt Hughes was about to push it open when Bob seized his arm and put his finger on his lips. Then he pulled his uncle back several steps.

"That door was locked when I left," he whispered. "Someone's been in my room."

Merritt Hughes looked startled.

"Sure?" he whispered.

"There's no question about it," replied Bob.

"Then keep back and let me go ahead."   It

was a whispered command that Bob dared not disobey and he saw his uncle reach under his left arm and draw a revolver from a shoulder holster.

They stepped close to the wall and again advanced toward the door, treading silently on the heavy carpet of the corridor. There was no sound of anyone moving about inside the room, but Merritt Hughes did not believe in taking unnecessary chances.

After listening a moment at the door, he reached out with one foot and gave it a hard shove inward, at the same time leaping into the doorway, gun in hand and ready for action.

It was a breathless moment for Bob until he saw his uncle lower the weapon and nod to him.

"Come here and take a look at your room."

CHAPTER XVI

IN BOB'S ROOM

✼

Bob stepped through the doorway, and stopped involuntarily. The interior of his room looked like a young cyclone had been turned loose on a spring afternoon. Every drawer in the dresser had been pulled out and its contents dumped on the floor, the bedding was strewn about the room and the mattress had been ripped open and even his clothes had been taken out of the closet and scattered about.

"Friends of yours must have been disappointed because you weren't at home," said his uncle.

Bob sat down in a chair and took another look around. Nothing in the room had been spared. Even the pictures had been taken off the walls and the backs ripped out.

He looked down at a coat which had been dropped beside the chair. The pockets had been turned inside out and the lining of the garment had been torn and ripped. The coat was ruined and Bob felt hot tears of anger welling into his eyes. His fists doubled up involuntarily. Someone would have to pay for this, he told himself.

Merritt Hughes touched his shoulder.

"Keep your chin up, Bob. This is kind of tough and it looks plain malicious to me, but your time will come. I'm just wondering why all of this attention is being centered on you. I can't make myself believe that they are trying to get even with you because you spoiled the game last night."

"But I didn't. The paper is missing."

"Yes, it's gone from the files, but they may not have their hands on it yet. Sure you made a thorough search down below the building last night? It couldn't have been caught in the shrubbery?"

"I'm sure about that. We went over every inch of space and found half of the gum wrappers in Washington," replied Bob.

"I wish I could feel sure that the paper has not gotten into the hands of the men who are after it. From what's gone on today I'm inclined to believe there has been a slip somewhere.

We know the paper is missing from the files but we're not sure that the man who took it was able to deliver it outside before you caught him."

"I don't think he did. His only chance would have been to have dropped it from the window and that would have been too risky."

"He might have placed it in a marked container of some kind and have had a confederate waiting below," suggested the federal agent.

"That's possible, but when Arthur Jacobs and I searched last night we couldn't even find fresh footprints under the windows. Of course there were some near the window where the guard was trussed up, but if the paper had been dropped in a container, there should have been footprints directly below."

"The rain might have erased them."

"I doubt it. The ground under the shrubbery is unusually soft and I noticed how deep our own prints were."

Merritt Hughes sat down on the bed and it was a long time before he asked Bob another question.

"What do you think about Tully? Could he possibly have taken that paper out of the file?"

"Not unless he was a magician and I don't think Tully would do a thing like that. He's wild and headstrong, but he wouldn't go that far. Why that's working against Uncle Sam!"

"Certainly, but some people aren't bothered by scruples like that. Well, if we're sure the paper wasn't tossed out the window, it narrows down to three people—the man you caught, Tully and yourself."

"But I wouldn't take that paper," smiled Bob.

"Of course not. I know that and so does Waldo Edgar, or he wouldn't have made you a provisional agent. But Condon Adams is as anxious to solve this case as I am and he may try to hang something around your neck. Remember, that only three of you were in the room and that paper disappeared in some manner."

"I hadn't thought of it in that way," reflected Bob. "It does put me in a pretty serious light."

"That's why I have been so anxious that you be assigned to work with me on this case. I had a long talk with Edgar this morning. I'd told him of your ambition to eventually join the service and pointed out that you might well prove invaluable as an inside man on this case. He agreed with me and of course when Condon Adams put up about the same kind of a proposition in behalf of Tully, he couldn't say no."

"I'd like to know where Adams gets all his pull," said Bob.

"Part of it is due to ability and part of it to powerful political friends," explained his uncle. "The senator from Adams' home state is high up in administration circles and in addition is a firm friend of this department. He's helped get us the additional appropriations we've needed to expand and equip the department properly and of course the chief can't ignore that when Adams puts the pressure on."

"I suppose not," admitted Bob, "but it seems unfair to the other men who have no political friends."

"His is about the only case in the department in which that is true," said his uncle. "But he's competent, too. Don't mistake that. I'll have to keep on my toes if I run this radio mystery down before he does."

"All of which means that I am the inside man for you while Tully is to serve his uncle in whatever inside capacity he can in our department," said Bob. "I can see where there is going to be some intense rivalry."

"Well, either Adams or myself should benefit by it," smiled the federal agent. "Only don't kill each other trying to dig out facts and get them to us first. Now we'd better find out what we can about the invasion here. How about your landlords?"

"They're down in Virginia on a vacation. The only person likely to know anything about this is the janitor," explained Bob.

"Take me down to him," directed his uncle.

Bob looked ruefully at the room. There wasn't a whole lot that could be salvaged, for his clothing was ruined and one of the suits had been practically new. He could see his savings account going down almost to the vanishing point.

They stepped out into the hall and Bob started to lock the door.

"Wait a minute. I want a look at that door-knob," said his uncle. He took a small but powerful glass from his coat pocket and examined the doorknob. When he stood up he shook his head.

"Whoever opened that door was wearing gloves. That means if they were that smart there isn't much use to check over the interior of the rooms for fingerprints."

"Any sign of the door being forced?" asked Bob.

"No. A skeleton key must have been used. Lead on; we'll see the janitor now."

They found the janitor in the basement and when Bob explained their mission he readily assented to answer their questions.

"Strangers?" he said, repeating the question the federal agent asked. "Yes, a couple of them called about an hour ago. They wanted to know where Mr. Houston lived and I took them up to the third floor back. They said they had been sent to get some papers he had left at home."

"How did they get in?" the question shot from the lips of the federal agent.

"Why, they had a key," explained the janitor. "One of them said Mr. Houston had given them his key. It worked all right and I didn't think any more about it. I was having trouble with the furnace smoking, so I came right back down here."

"And left them alone in Bob's room?" the agent pressed.

"That's right. They seemed to know what they were about."

"How long did they stay up there?"

"I don't rightly know. I went up to that floor a few minutes ago, but no one was in sight then. Maybe they were there half an hour; maybe only five minutes."

"What did they look like?"

The janitor scratched his head.

"Well, now, I didn't pay a whole lot of attention to them. One of them was a lot taller than the other one, though."

A premonition had been growing on Bob and he couldn't repress his question.

"Did the taller one have red hair?" he asked.

"Come to think of it, he did," replied the janitor.

"And the shorter one; was there a scar on his forehead?"

"That's right. Friends of yours, of course?"

"Well, not exactly friends," said Bob.

"Remember anything else about them?" asked Merritt Hughes.

"Not right now, anyhow," said the janitor and they left him to return to his work while they went outdoors.

Merritt Hughes was the first to speak.

"I guess there is no question about the identity of your visitors. They are the same ones who attempted to kidnap you. What's the reason for all of your popularity?"

Bob shook his head.

"I only wish I knew," he said. "Believe me, it is no fun to have your room torn apart like that. Why they ruined my clothes and it's going to be mighty costly getting them repaired."

"I'll help you out if you're pinched for money," volunteered his uncle, reaching for his billfold.

But Bob waved the offer aside.

"Thanks, but I'll get along all right. If I ever catch up with those fellows they'll have to get their fists into action pretty fast if they want to escape a thorough drubbing."

"I don't blame you a bit for feeling that way. But we've got to get along. I have an appointment with one of the army's chief radio engineers in less than fifteen minutes and I want you to sit in."

They signalled for a cab and started for the meeting which was to reveal some startling information on Bob's first case.

Chapter XVII

THE RADIO SECRET

★

MERRITT HUGHES leaned back in the seat as the cab darted in and out of the heavy traffic on the avenue.

"All of the breaks have been against us so far," he mused, half to himself and half to Bob, "but we're bound to find something coming our way soon."

"I'm anxious to see the fellow who is being held at the police station," said Bob. "Surely you'll be able to get some information out of him."

"Remember you're working on this case, too. Better say 'we' instead of 'you' when you're talking about it. This is the firm of Hughes and Houston, working for Uncle Sam on a radio mystery."

Their cab pulled up in front of the War Department and they entered and hastened to an upper floor where the federal agent rapped

sharply on a door marked "Major Francis Mc-
Creary, Private."

"Come in," a heavy voice on the other side
rumbled and Merritt Hughes opened the door.

Bob, looking in, saw a heavy man, a huge
thatch of hair bristling over his forehead, at a
flat-topped desk. He rose as they entered.

"Hello, Hughes," greeted the major. "Right
on time." He nodded toward a desk clock.

"Made it with nothing to spare," grinned Bob's
uncle. Then he added, "Major, I want you to
know my nephew, Bob Houston. He's working
with me on this case. Bob's the man who captured our radio thief last night and I'm counting
on him as a valuable inside man in the department over there."

"Glad to meet you," boomed the major, offering a warm handclasp. "Are you in the Department of Justice?"

Bob started to reply but his uncle spoke first.

"He's in the filing division right now, but he's
also a provisional agent and I'm expecting he'll
join the service permanently."

The major shuffled several papers on his desk
and picked up one.

"Here's a copy of the paper stolen last night," he said. "I know you want the gist of its importance and why so much interest attaches to it."

He waved them toward chairs and dropped back in his own swivel seat, which he filled to overflowing with his generous bulk.

"We've been making some real strides in our army radio development," he went on, "and some other powers have been watching us closely. There's no need to mention names right now until suspicion definitely points to a nation. What we have actually perfected in recent weeks is a workable radio control for robot operated bombing planes."

He paused a moment to let the significance of his statement sink in.

Bob knew its importance. Of course there had long been talk that such a device was possible, but it had never been perfected so far as he knew. Its value as a weapon of destruction was tremendous for airplanes loaded with high explosives could be dispatched over great distances and then made to drop their deadly cargoes upon a radio signal.

Bob glanced at his uncle. Merritt Hughes was sitting on the edge of his chair, waiting for the army officer to continue.

Major McCreary cleared his throat and Bob sensed that he was laboring under a definite strain.

"This project has been a pet of mine for years. I've encountered one discouragement after another and it was only two months ago that I struck the right track. Since then my developments have been almost sensational." He paused a moment as though fearing they might feel he was bragging about his own accomplishments.

"Actual tests last week proved the practicability of my invention and I then set it down in detail for final filing. Of course we knew that other powers were aware of the line along which the experiments had been carried out, but our real source of worry was that they might get their hands on the actual details of operation. For that reason it was decided to file the material in various sections and to make no special fuss about it."

"And the paper stolen last night was the first section of your file?" asked Merritt Hughes, restraining his eagerness no longer.

The army officer nodded.

"Right. It was the original. The one on my desk is a copy. The other originals are in a safe in this building."

"Is there enough information on the first section which was stolen to reveal your plan in full?" asked Bob.

"That's something that would depend upon the cleverness of the men into whose hands it is delivered. There is one European power whose radio experts are well advanced along the line on which I have been working. If this document is delivered into their hands, there is a good chance that it contains information which would be of value to them."

"But so far we have no idea who is behind the theft last night," said the federal agent. "Have you any hunches?"

Major McCreary shook his head.

"Nothing strong enough to give you any leads. But I'll let you know the minute anything develops. In the meantime, make every effort to recover this paper. Once it passes beyond the boundaries of this country it may fall into the hands of men smart enough and unscrupulous enough to learn its meaning and put it to their own selfish use. It is a secret which would give them unlimited powers of destruction."

After they had left Major McCreary's office Bob looked at his uncle.

"What next?" he asked.

"To the police station to interview that prisoner without any further loss of time," was the decision.

The station was some distance away and they took a taxi. Before they had gone three blocks the hooting of police sirens fairly filled the air and their driver was forced to pull far over to the right as radio cars went racing past, each driver tense at his wheel and the other officer ready with a shotgun in his lap.

"Something big's broken," said the federal agent. "Be just my luck to have it an angle on this case. Oh well, we might as well go on to the station and see what we can dig out of your friend."

As they reached the police station another squad car rushed away, its siren screaming a warning to traffic.

Merritt Hughes fairly tossed the cab fare at the driver and with Bob at his heels, ran into the building. The federal agent knew the desk sergeant and directed his questions at him.

"What's up, Barney? Bank been robbed?"

"Just about as bad. Someone slugged one of your agents and made a break. Matter of fact, I guess it was a friend of yours."

"Quit kidding, Barney. What happened?"

"The fellow you caught last night was being questioned by Condon Adams when all of a sudden he ups and smashes Adams a nasty crack on the chin, grabs his gun, and legs it out the door. We've got every squad car in town out hunting for him."

Bob felt his own heart sink for he knew that unless the fugitive was recaptured, their hopes for a real break in the radio mystery were slim.

CHAPTER XVIII

MEAGER HOPES

★

MERRITT HUGHES stared hard at the police sergeant as though he dared not believe the officer's words.

"Say that again, Barney. There must be some mistake."

"There was," grinned the sergeant. "Condon Adams made a mistake in questioning that fellow alone. Things certainly happened fast and furiously around here."

The federal agent shook his head.

"We're certainly not getting the breaks in this case," he growled. "Where's Adams?"

"He's out with one of the radio patrols."

"Have any idea where this fellow went when he made his break from the station here?"

"He forced a passing motorist to pick him up, but we didn't even get a good description of the car. Oh, it was a smooth job."

Merritt Hughes turned to his nephew and Bob saw an expression of almost despair in his face. Then it was gone in a moment, and in its place was a set look of determination which Bob had often seen when his uncle was working on a big case.

"Anything I can do to help you here?" the federal agent asked the desk sergeant.

"Not a thing, unless this fellow comes back and tries to steal the station."

"Then we'll go along to the hospital and have a talk with the guard who was attacked last night."

As they left the police station they could hear the echo of the sirens in the distance.

"Think he'll get away?" asked Bob, who had spoken only one or twice during the entire time they had been in the station.

"I'm afraid so, especially since the police have no description of the car he commandeered," replied Merritt Hughes.

When they reached the hospital, they were shown immediately to the room where the guard was a patient. He was a middle-aged man, his dark hair streaked with grey and there was a bandage around his forehead where he had received a particularly painful blow from his assailant.

"Can he be interviewed?" the federal agent asked the nurse on duty in the room.

"If he doesn't talk too long," she replied.

Bob glimpsed the chart at the foot of the bed and learned that guard's name was Max Chervinka, and that he was fifty-three years old.

Merritt Hughes sat down beside the bed, while Bob, behind him, leaned against the wall.

"I'll ask all the questions," the federal agent told the guard. "Don't talk unless you have to. Just nod a little in answer and that will do. Understand?"

The guard smiled and nodded.

"Had you noticed anything suspicious about the building recently?"

The answer was negative. Then the federal agent plunged into his questions, how had the attack taken place, what did the man look like, was there more than one, had he seen anything of a paper which might have been tossed from an upper window?

The answers were definite. The guard could

not describe his assailant, as far as he knew there had been only one man, and he had not seen anything of a paper thrown from a window.

"Have you ever been offered anything to let anyone in the building who had no business there?" The federal agent rapped out this question sharply and Bob knew that his uncle attached great importance to the answer.

"Never!" The guard's reply, though in a weak voice, was definite. "There was never any trouble until last night," he added.

The nurse reentered the room, noticed the bright eyes and the flushed cheeks of her patient, and spoke to the federal agents.

"I think he's had all of the exertion he can stand for a while," she said. "Later, perhaps this evening, you might call again if you like."

"Has anyone else been here?" asked Merritt Hughes.

"Not yet."

"Then don't allow anyone to see him unless he can identify himself as a Department of Justice agent," he instructed.

When they were down on the main floor, Bob spoke.

"Why did you instruct the nurse like that?"

"Just playing safe. We know that the guard didn't see enough of his assailant to identify him, but other members of that gang don't know that. There is no use in exposing that fellow to any unnecessary risks."

When they were outside once more, Bob voiced another question.

"What do you want me to do now?"

"Better go down to your own office and step back into the routine. But keep your eyes open. Listen to everything that is going on, but don't let anyone get anything out of you. Phone me before you leave this afternoon to go home. I don't want you gallivanting around this town all alone. The next time some of your 'friends' may come along and there may not be a fence and a thicket of barberry handy."

"I'll take a taxi home; you won't need to come for me," protested Bob.

"You're not going to take a taxi home and you're not going home. Until this thing is cleared up you're going to stay with me. Then if anyone decides to pay us a visit in the middle of the night we'll give them a surprise."

"Let me know if anything big breaks," urged Bob, and his uncle promised to do this.

After their parting, Bob walked down the street alone. A police car sped by, but its siren was not sounding an alarm, and Bob wondered if the rush of the first chase for the escaped prisoner was over.

As he hurried toward the archives building, he pondered the events of the last 24 hours. It seemed almost incredible that so much could have happened; that he could have been involved in so many different and exciting things. And now he was a federal agent. True he was only on provisional duty, but if he made good, there was an excellent chance that he would become a permanent member of the great crime-fighting organization.

His uncle had been right—so far the breaks had all been against them and now the one man on whom they had been counting for information had slipped away. But Bob couldn't help a grin as he thought of the chagrin which Condon Adams must be suffering now. It would be hard to explain that escape from the very heart of a police station.

Bob turned into the building where his own office was located and took the elevator to the top floor.

When he entered the office he almost bumped into Arthur Jacobs, the filing chief.

"Any news?" asked Jacobs anxiously and Bob shook his head.

"What about the prisoner captured last night?"

· "Don't you know?" asked Bob.

"Know what?" demanded the filing chief.

"He just escaped from the police station."

"Then we're sunk," groaned the filing chief. "That means that paper is gone for good and I'll bet my job is too."

"Oh, I wouldn't say that. Give the federal men a chance."

"But they've had nearly 24 hours," wailed the chubby Jacobs.

"You can't expect them to do miracles in that length of time," cautioned Bob.

Before the filing chief could reply, the door swung inward and Tully Ross hurried in.

His face was flushed and he appeared to be laboring under some great excitement.

Arthur Jacobs looked at his watch.

"You might just as well have taken the whole day off," he snapped.

"Well, maybe I will," retorted Tully.

"I guess that's about enough from you," said the filing chief. "I'll find plenty of extra work for you to do and you may change your attitude and show a little respect."

A dark wave of color swept over Tully's face and Bob saw his fists clench. He stepped closer to Jacobs.

"I'll get here just when I please," he stormed, "and don't think I'm going to let you boss me around. I'm a federal agent now and I'm working on a big case. Don't you forget that."

But in spite of the bravado, Arthur Jacobs stood his ground.

"I don't care what you are," he replied. "As far as I know you're nothing but a clerk in my department and you'll get to work on time and you'll be respectful or you'll get another job."

"If you don't believe I'm a federal agent, ask Bob; he'll tell you."

The filing chief turned to Bob.

"Tully is right. I saw him sworn into the service today," said Bob. He was glad that Jacobs had not asked him about his own position.

Tully seemed satisfied and his anger subsided when Jacobs once more told him to go to his desk and start work.

Bob glanced at the other clerks in the room. All of them had been covertly watching the entire proceedings. Bob felt that they were all trustworthy, but he felt better in knowing that they were not aware that he was a federal agent. Such knowledge might have spoiled any later efforts of his to gain information from them.

CHAPTER XIX

THE MISSING PAPER

★

THE affairs of the filing office gradually returned to routine with Bob and Tully
once more at their desks. There was a
tremendous amount of work to be done, for
hundreds upon hundreds of papers had been removed from their usual places in the mêlée of the
night before. Bob realized that it would take
days for them all to be restored to their places
and he rather hoped, as he contemplated the long
and tedious task, that his uncle would have work
for him to do that would take him outside the
office.

As the afternoon waned Bob tried to analyze
the character of the other clerks in the office. He
had known them casually for more than a year
now, but until this time he had never really tried
to probe into their inner characters.

It was a task that he was particularly well fitted to do, for he had a rare gift of discernment of character and anything untrue in another usually sounded an alarm bell in Bob's mind.

One by one he checked them off his list of possible suspects in connection with the disappearance of the radio paper. Could one of them have tipped off anyone outside? It was an unpleasant possibility, but Bob knew that in his new work he would be up against many unpleasant things.

The list narrowed down until Bob's eyes rested on Tully's broad shoulders. The other was hunched over his desk, apparently gazing through a nearby window and certainly not much concerned with the work on the desk in front of him.

Was Tully linked up with the mystery? Could he have been the one inside who had learned of the arrival of the precious paper and given the information to someone outside?

Bob didn't want to believe that, yet he had checked all of the others off his list. His eyes rested on Arthur Jacobs, the filing chief. Could it have been Jacobs? It was possible, but Bob scouted serious consideration of the thought, for

Jacobs' heart was too much in his work and his pride was too great for such a deed.

Bob felt up against a blank wall. It was his job to sit tight in the office on the supposition that someone inside must have given out information. He felt now that there was little chance that this had been the case. There were plenty of other loopholes for the information to leak out and Bob was convinced that it must have leaked before the paper came into the filing office.

At five o'clock the other clerks left their desks, but Tully, Bob and the filing chief lingered in the office.

Jacobs spoke to Tully.

"I don't care what you're doing outside this office," he said, "but as long as you're here and at your desk you'll have to work. I don't believe you did five minutes work this afternoon."

Tully's eyes dropped and he studied the toes of his shoes. His voice was heavy when he spoke.

"I know I didn't get much work done," he said. "But I was so blamed excited over being a federal agent and then trying to figure out how this information could have leaked out. I'll be back to earth again tomorrow."

"I'm glad of that for we need your help in getting this mess straightened out."

Tully nodded and went on, while Bob hesitated.

"I wanted just a word with you alone," he told the filing chief. "I didn't say anything earlier, but I'm also working on this case as a provisional federal agent. That means I'm on probation. If I make good on this case there may be a permanent job waiting for me."

"I rather thought you might be," smiled Jacobs, "after Tully blurted out that he was a special agent. I kind of put two and two together and it looked like it would be mighty strange if Tully were selected and not you."

"It may be necessary for me to be away from the office at various times," went on Bob, "but if I can't get word to you, my uncle will see that you are advised."

"Anything that really looks like a clue turned up?" asked Jacobs.

Bob shook his head.

"Not as far as I know, and I guess if there

had been I wouldn't be at liberty to tell you."

Jacobs put on his coat.

"Coming down tonight?"

"I've some routine I can get out of the way," replied Bob. "I'll have lunch nearby and will be able to get through in a couple of hours."

"I should come back, but I'm all in. Don't work too late."

The filing chief stepped out of the office and closed the door behind him and Bob was left alone in the long, high-ceilinged office. The room was in heavy shadows already, for the day had been cloudy and twilight had come early. He turned on the light over his desk, decided that he was hungry, snapped it off, put on his coat and left the office. At the door he turned and made sure that the room was securely locked. Then he walked rapidly down the corridor, turned, and signalled for an elevator.

Bob was walking through the main doors when someone hailed him and he saw his uncle.

"Going to eat?" asked Merritt Hughes.

"Just about half a ton of food," grinned Bob. "It seems ages since I had anything, yet it was only a few hours ago."

"Charge that up to excitement," replied his uncle, as they strode along together.

"Any news of the man who broke out of the police station?" There was a real note of anxiety in Bob's voice.

"Not a word. He must have been a magician. The police are still combing the city, but I doubt if they'll find him. He belongs to too clever a gang."

"But where could he hide so securely in Washington?"

"An embassy, possibly," shrugged the federal agent.

Bob's eyes widened. It had never occurred to him that a representative of a foreign government would give shelter to a criminal. Yet he knew that any one of half a dozen foreign powers would give a great deal to possess the new radio secrets.

"Don't take that suggestion too seriously," warned Merritt Hughes, who guessed the trend of Bob's thoughts.

He leaned closer to Bob. "This case is causing all kinds of trouble. The entire War Department is in a furore and I hear special intelligence officers are being assigned to see if they can't ferret it out."

"Does that mean they don't think the Justice Department capable of solving the mystery?" asked Bob.

"Not exactly that, I guess. It simply means that this case is of such tremendous importance that everything the government can do will be done in its solution."

They turned into a quiet restaurant and selected a table well to the rear where they could talk without danger of being overheard for there were only a few diners in the place.

"Have you seen Condon Adams?" asked Bob.

The federal agent shook his head.

"I hear he's having a pretty hard time of it. The chief had him in on the carpet and gave him a going over for letting this fellow slip away from him. But it could have happened to anyone. If we'd gotten there first instead of Adams, we might have been the victims."

They ordered their dinners and Bob leaned across the table.

"I've been trying to figure out everyone in the office," he said, "and I can't find a single one on whom you can pin any suspicion. The leak about that paper must have come from outside before the paper reached us."

"That's possible," nodded his uncle.

"Remember that another office was rifled before our own was visited," said Bob. "That should indicate that the marauder had none too clear information on where to look for the paper."

"Now you've hit a point I've been considering. The more I think about it the more convinced I become that the leak came before the paper reached your filing room. That means our job will be complicated. Maybe we'll get a break one of these days."

Dinner was served and they ate heartily, ignoring for the time the case that had enfolded both of them in its mysterious tangle.

The dinner at an end, Bob leaned back in his chair and shoved his hands in his coat pockets. The fingers of his right hand crinkled a stiff sheet of paper and he drew it out and placed it on the table.

It was not an unusual sheet, at first glance, being about eight inches wide and eleven inches long, but it was of heavy material, probably a pure rag paper.

But it was not the paper that caught and held Bob's attention. It was the crest of the war department which was centered at the top of the page.

Merritt Hughes saw Bob staring at the paper and looked at his nephew curiously.

"What's the matter, Bob? Forget to file something this afternoon?"

When Bob did not answer at once, he reached over and picked up the paper. It was his turn to stare at the sheet and his eyes widened as he looked up at his nephew.

"Great heavens, Bob. Where did this come from?"

Bob shook his head.

"I haven't any idea. I put my hands in my pockets just now and the paper was in the right hand pocket."

"But you know what this is?"

Bob nodded. "Yes, I know. It's the missing paper with the radio secrets."

CHAPTER XX

ON A LONELY STREET

★

UNCLE and nephew stared at each other across the litter of dishes and for a moment neither was able to speak.

"Bob, Bob, how did you get mixed up in this thing? What have you done?" There was anxiety and agony in every word that came from the lips of the federal agent.

Bob's eyes widened.

"But surely you don't think I took this? I couldn't have done that."

His uncle waved his hands impatiently.

"No, no, Bob. Of course that wasn't what I meant. I spoke hastily. You're clean enough in this thing. What I want to know is how did that paper get into your coat pocket and how long has it been there."

"I only wish I knew," retorted Bob, the color surging back into his cheeks.

He stared steadily at the paper on the table before him. It was incredible that it could have been in his coat pocket all during the long hours of the frantic search for it. Yet it must have been, for there had been no opportunity for anyone to slip it into his coat recently.

"I think the discovery of the paper in your pocket explains the mysterious attacks which have been aimed at you," said his uncle slowly. "Certainly it was the reason for the rifling of your room and the attempt to kidnap you this morning. What a dumb-bell I was not to have guessed something like this before. It's as plain as day now."

"I wish I could see it that way," replied Bob, shaking his head.

"The paper has been in your pocket ever since you encountered that marauder in the office last night. During the tussle he slipped it into your coat pocket when he realized that his capture was inevitable."

"That sounds plausible," agreed Bob. "Why didn't I search my own clothes?"

"Because that was the last place in the world we would have surmised that paper had been hidden. What chumps we have been." The federal agent look gloomy.

"Well, I guess we might as well get going. We'll report this directly to the chief and see what he has to say about it."

"Will he be on the job during the evening?"

"When a case like this breaks he practically lives in his office. He'll be there all right."

They left the restaurant, secured a taxi, and drove rapidly toward the department of justice building.

Bob, catching the reflection of lights behind them in the mirror at the front, looked back.

"Someone's following us," he said.

The federal agent turned quickly. There was no mistake. A car several hundred feet to the rear was making every turn their own machine took.

Merritt Hughes leaned ahead and spoke to the driver.

"We're being trailed. Step on it. I'll take care of any officers who try to stop us."

"Nothing doin', mister. I'm not getting myself into trouble. We're stopping right here."

The driver slammed on the brakes and swung

his car toward the curb, but a curt command from Bob's uncle stopped him.

"Get this car under way. I'm a federal agent and I'm in no mood to have you playing any tricks. Wheel this buggy for the Department of Justice building and make it snappy." At the same time he thrust the little emblem of his office under the driver's nose.

The motor of the taxi roared as the driver tramped on the accelerator and their vehicle leaped ahead, widening the distance between the car which was trailing them. They took a corner so fast the tires screeched in protest and Bob wondered whether the other machine would be able to make the turn.

Looking back he saw the car swing wildly, veer toward the far side of the street, and finally straighten out in pursuit of them.

"You seem to spell 'trouble' with capital letters," said the federal agent as he joined Bob in peering out the window. "Maybe you'd better give me that paper. They know you've got it and if we get in a jam they'll try and get it away from you."

Bob handed over the paper and his uncle slipped it into a small leather portfolio which he carried in an inside pocket of his coat.

The taxi swung wildly around another corner and the brakes screeched as a string of red lights barred their way. The street was undergoing repairs.

The driver of their vehicle jammed on his brakes just as the pursuing machine lurched around the corner.

"Keep on going!" cried Bob's uncle, grabbing the driver by the shoulder and shaking him roughly. "Keep on!"

It was a command the driver dared not disobey, and their car leaped ahead once more, aimed straight at the first of the red lights.

Their headlights revealed a wooden barrier, but there was no stopping now and the taxi crashed into the stringers. Several red lights were bowled over as the barrier went down. Then they were bouncing along over the uneven paving, the wheels dropping into deep ruts.

Bob turned and looked behind them. The pursuing car had stopped at the barrier and he could see men leaping out. It was evident that they intended to pursue the chase, even on foot.

"I'm wrecking this car," cried the taxi driver in protest as they struck a particularly deep rut.

"Keep going; don't worry about the car!" cried Merritt Hughes. "We've got to get out of this trap."

The engine of the taxi groaned in protest of the punishment which it was undergoing, but it labored on, dragging the heavy vehicle out of one hole and into another.

Bob kept his eyes on the pursuers, who were now plainly revealed in the lights from the other car. They seemed to be gaining on the struggling taxi.

"We'd better take a chance on foot," he warned his uncle.

"It's only a little ways to the end of this construction work. If we can get that far, we'll soon outdistance them," replied Merritt Hughes. "If we get stalled, make a break for it. Don't worry about me. Once you get clear go directly to the Department of Justice and report in person to Waldo Edgar."

"But we'll have a better chance together," protested Bob.

"No. We'll go it alone," his uncle decided.

"That will confuse them and one of us is bound to get away."

"But how about the radio secret?"

"We've got to chance that. But remember that you are the one they'll be after. Maybe that's putting you on the spot, but I've got to do it now. It's our only chance."

The headlights of the taxi showed the end of the construction work. A smooth street was less than 100 feet ahead of them, but Bob thought the remainder of the distance they must go looked even rougher than that portion of the street they had negotiated so far.

He looked behind again. Several dim shadows, the men chasing them, were dodging down the street. He doubted if they were gaining now.

The taxi dropped into a deep rut and the engine groaned. The driver shifted gears with a clash that racked the entire car and the wheels spun in the rut. Then they shot into reverse, but the wheels couldn't climb out.

"We're stuck!" cried the driver. "I'm unloading."

With a single motion of his hand he struck the ignition switch and the motor, overheated and steaming, sputtered and died. The headlights also went out and Bob saw the now dim bulk of the cab driver leap away from the car and vanish.

"Get out, Bob. Duck and keep low. Make for the side of the street. Here's where we separate."

The order was accompanied by a firm shove toward the door and then Bob was rolling in the street, for he had missed his step and fallen. He heard the door on the other side of the cab open and knew that his uncle had made his escape at least for the time.

Chapter XXI

SHOTS IN THE NIGHT

★

THE street was long, flanked by what appeared to be warehouses, and there were street lights only at the ends of the block. For at least 400 feet in the middle there was no light and it was in this dismal area that Bob and his uncle were trapped.

A pile of construction materials offered the first shelter for Bob and he ducked behind this.

From this shelter, he listened for some sound from the men who had been pursuing them. He did not have long to wait for sharp voices could be heard a little further back along the street.

"The taxi's stalled," someone said. "Spread out and let them have it if they make a break. We've got to get them to be sure we'll get the paper."

Bob, behind the pile of construction materials, heard someone pounding down the street.

The beam from a flashlight shot through the night and focused on the taxi driver.

"Snap off that light!" came a tense command. "That's only the driver. Let him go."

"He'll bring the cops on us," came a sharp protest, but the first voice came back tartly.

"Let him. We'll be out of here long before he can get his nerve back and talk to the police. Spread out, I tell you. We've got to move fast. If they break for the far end of the street we'll see them under the street lights. There's no place they can hide at each side."

The last words confirmed Bob's fears. That meant that there was no shelter in the buildings which flanked the street. This time there was no friendly hedge into which he could leap. He would have been glad to have risked the barberry thorns again if he had only had the chance.

The taxi was less than twenty feet away and Bob knew that the men hunting for him and his uncle would reach it in a few more seconds. Then one of the first places where they would search would be the pile of bricks and timbers behind which he had sought refuge.

Bob moved away cautiously, a plan of action

quickly forming in his mind. He would get as far away as possible, then make some noise to attract their attention. It seemed like a good move for by concentrating their attention on himself, he would provide an opportunity for his uncle to slip away unnoticed and the radio document could be delivered safely back to the war department.

Bob felt a nervous tension gripping his entire body. It was as though the very night was alive to the danger which filled the deserted street. The pounding footsteps of the taxi driver gradually died away and only Bob and his uncle and three unknown pursuers were in the street.

A flashlight gleamed for a moment at the taxi as the beam sought the interior.

"Nothing here," Bob heard someone mutter as he backed away from the sheltering pile of materials.

A piece of board crunched under his feet and he stumbled and half fell to the ground.

"What's that!" the exclamation was sharp and commanding and a beam of light swung toward him.

Bob forgot caution and scuttled away on his

hands and feet, dodging behind the piles of dirt which had been heaped indiscriminately around the street.

The flashlight seemed to be playing a game of hide and seek with him, for not once did the beam strike him and he found temporary shelter again behind a pile of bricks.

But the sanctuary was not to last for long. From the voices near the taxi, Bob knew that at least three men were after them and as he listened he heard a command that sent a chill racing along his spine.

"Don't shoot unless you have to. But let them have it if it looks like they're going to get away."

Bob remembered that his uncle had a gun. That was some consolation. He would have to depend upon his fists for self protection and right now both hands were sore and aching from his encounter earlier in the day with the thorns of the barberry.

The young federal agent crouched close to the ground listening for some sound that might indicate the whereabouts of his uncle. He only knew that Merritt Hughes had dodged out the other side of the taxi. Since then there had been no sign or noise to reveal where he had sought shelter.

Bob strained his eyes, but the darkness in the middle of the block was intense. Perhaps, after all, that was a blessing for it gave them a better opportunity to hide and made the task of the searchers all the harder.

Impatient and cramped from hiding behind the pile of bricks, Bob moved away. He was determined to escape from the trap into which they had fallen and he decided that by working his way back along the street toward the car which had been used by their pursuers might offer the best avenue of escape.

A bold thought occurred. It might even be possible to seize their car and make his own escape.

Bob, crouching low, crept along the street, at times almost crawling. It wasn't a pleasant task, but he was steadily putting distance between himself and the stalled taxi, where he knew the hunt for his uncle and himself was being concentrated.

The young federal agent stumbled over a timber and sprawled headlong on the dirt.

To Bob it sounded as though the noise of his fall must have echoed and re-echoed along the street. He remained motionless, almost breathless on the ground, waiting for the pursuit to swing toward him. But evidently the noise of his tumble was not as great as he had feared and the hunt continued near the taxi.

Bob continued his cautious advance toward the car which had brought their pursuers. He was not certain whether anyone had been left to guard the machine and he moved carefully as he neared the vehicle.

He was now at least 200 feet from the stalled taxi, and he had no desire to give an alarm which would bring the others swarming toward him.

Bob now had decided what he would do when he reached the car. In turning it about he would race the engine, which would be sure to attract the attention of the men seeking his uncle and allow him to escape from the far end of the street. There should be ample time for Bob to maneuver the car about and get it started back down the street before he could be overhauled.

The young federal agent was less than twenty

feet from the car, close enough to hear the soft purring of its powerful engine, when a gun blazed from behind him and the echoes of a shot resounded between the buildings which flanked the street.

CHAPTER XXII

THE LONE STRUGGLE

★

A<small>LL</small> thoughts of escaping in the car vanished from Bob's mind on the echoes of the shot, which meant that his uncle had been discovered, that he was a target for gunfire from the guns of their pursuers.

The young federal agent swung about in his tracks and started back down the street, stumbling over the piles of debris as he raced forward, forgetful now of any danger to himself and thinking only of his chance to help his uncle protect the precious paper which was in his possession.

From the vicinity of the stalled taxi cab guns were barking steadily now and Bob paused.

The scarlet flashes marked the night and the sharp reports from the guns rang back and forth between the high-walled street. Bob counted three guns in action, all directed toward a darker mass near the far end of the street.

Then another gun joined in the fusilade, this time from what apparently was a pile of debris and from its heavy roar Bob knew that it was his uncle's automatic.

Merritt Hughes, who had made his way cautiously toward the far end of the street, had been discovered just before he could make a final break to safety. After the first shot from the guns of his pursuers, he had taken refuge behind a pile of bricks and concrete slabs, where he was ready to make a determined resistance.

If he could stand off the attack for several minutes, a swarm of police, attracted by the gunfire, would descend upon them. But the men in the street were shooting carefully and spreading out, attempting to encircle him and force his surrender. They were moving rapidly, dodging so quickly that it was almost impossible to single them out in the shadows or to flip an accurate shot at them.

His ammunition was confined to the one clip in his gun and a spare clip in his coat pocket. It wouldn't last long in an encounter with three gunmen and every shot must be made to count.

A close shot, which struck a slab of concrete,

threw a fine cloud of dust into his eyes and blinded him for the moment. He wondered about Bob and whether he had been able to make his escape. If he hadn't before this, now surely, with all of the firing, he would be able to escape from the street. Perhaps he would even be able to lead the rescuing police which he felt sure would come soon.

But Bob, at the other end of the street, had his own ideas about the police and the need for a hasty rescue.

He paused in his mad dash down the block. Unarmed, he would be no match for the gun-men who were attempting to surround his uncle and obtain the paper.

A new plan formed in Bob's mind and he turned determinedly and headed for the car. It was a large and powerful sedan with a motor under its hood that equalled the power of a hundred and twenty horses.

There was no one in the car and Bob slid into the driver's seat. The doors were unusually high and heavy and he guessed that the car was bullet proof.

Bob reached for the headlight switch, then

thought better of it, and meshed the gears into low. He tramped on the throttle and the motor roared into action. With a lurch the heavy car plunged off the pavement and into the street which was undergoing repairs.

Bob would have liked to have used the headlights for they would have revealed the menace of hidden mounds of dirt and bricks and other construction materials, but to have switched them on would have made the car too easy a target for the gunmen.

Looking ahead, Bob saw the flashes of gunfire cease, as though the men who had been pulling the triggers were surprised and alarmed at the approach of the car.

Then there was a spurt of flame and something smacked hard against the windshield. He saw the glass shatter, but it did not break, and it gave him new confidence in the knowledge that the car was protected against bullets.

Now there were more flashes of crimson ahead of him and bullets spanked against the car. The glass of a headlight shattered into a thousand bits.

The big machine rammed into a pile of bricks and stalled. They were only half way down the block and Bob reversed quickly and backed the car away. With a sharp flip of the wheel he skirted the obstruction and once more roared ahead, the car gaining speed as it went along in second gear.

The roar of the motor was so loud that it drowned out the explosions of the guns.

Bob, watching for some sign of his uncle, thought he saw a form flit toward the side of the street, but he couldn't be sure.

The car bounced in and out of a ditch, the wheels spinning frantically and finally gaining enough traction to send it ahead once more.

The windshield, which had been struck four times, was a maze of shattered glass, and Bob could see only dimly the light which marked the end of the street. It was impossible to discern anything ahead of him and he turned on the headlights. It didn't matter much now, for the car was too large a target to miss.

But the lights failed to come on. Some bullet had probably clipped the wires, and Bob, his hands wrapped around the steering wheel, hung on grimly as the big car bounced along the uneven street.

There was a jarring crash and the big car, its wheels still spinning futilely, came to a stop. Bob was knocked against the steering wheel and his head reeled from the shock.

Dimly he heard someone jerk open the door and he tried to rally his dulled senses and put up a resistance, but a rough hand reached him and seized him by the shoulders. He was conscious that a light blazed suddenly in his face.

"It's the kid!" cried the heavy voice. "I'll search him. Get the other guy!"

Bob was jerked from the car and dropped to the ground. Once more the flashlight blazed, this time shielded behind a pile of bricks, and heavy hands went through his pockets.

As his head cleared, Bob realized his situation. Resistance right now to the search might give his uncle a few more precious minutes and Bob suddenly doubled up his knees and aimed a heavy kick at the man who was bending over him.

The maneuver caught the other unaware, and he stumbled back against the pile of bricks. The flashlight, dropping to the ground, went out.

"Give me a hand, over here! The kid's busted my flashlight," called the man Bob had kicked.

Then it felt as though a ton of beef had suddenly been dropped on him for the man who had captured him was trying to make sure that Bob would not squirm away from him. Just to make sure, he fell heavily on the young federal agent and Bob cried out in pain as the breath was forced from his lungs.

From the distance came the shrill siren of a police car.

"Hurry it up, over there," a voice called. "We've got to make a break out of here."

"Did you get the other guy?" demanded the man who was almost smothering Bob.

"Not yet."

On the echo of those words there came a shot and a cry.

"We've got him!"

Bob attempted to throw off his assailant, but a thousand stars seemed to descend upon him, police sirens mixed in with roaring motors and blazing guns and in spite of his efforts he dropped into a jumbled sleep.

Chapter XXIII

ANXIOUS HOURS

★

Mixed sounds penetrated through a maze of pain which filled Bob's head when he finally started to regain consciousness.

First of all there was the noise of police sirens which seemed to fill the night air with their shrieks.

Bob managed to raise himself up on one elbow just as a car careened around the corner and screeched to a stop. Men fairly poured from the car and Bob could see that each was heavily armed.

Lights gleamed in the disrupted street and Bob turned to look for the car which he had commandeered and from which he had been so roughly jerked. It had vanished and only the damaged taxi remained.

The echo of the gunfire had died away.

A beam of light focused on Bob and a sharp command followed.

"Don't move!"

At the moment Bob ached too much to care whether he ever moved. Someone came up from behind him and jerked him roughly to his feet.

"Snap a pair of handcuffs on this bird. We'll question him later." The command was from an officer who seemed to be in charge of the squad. From back down the street more sirens shrilled and Bob saw two more cars pull to a stop and officers unload hastily.

"Let me explain," protested Bob. "If you'll only look in the case inside my coat you'll find my identification papers. I'm a provisional federal agent."

One of the police laughed scornfully.

"That's a fine story. You're only a kid."

Bob was tired and worried now about his uncle. Hot tears of anger welled into his eyes and his voice trembled as he replied.

"You'd better take the time to make sure before you handcuff me. A federal agent has been kidnaped on this street and you'd better hunt for him instead of wasting your time on me."

"Who was kidnaped?" the question was asked by a newcomer who had joined the group.

"My uncle, Merritt Hughes," replied Bob. "He's in the department of justice."

"Say, maybe there is something to his story," chimed in another officer. "I know there is a federal agent by the name of Hughes."

"Then you'd better start looking for him. He was down at the end of this street a couple of minutes ago, the target for three gunmen. We were trapped here in the taxi that's deserted over there."

"Get busy, boys, and see what you can find," ordered the sergeant who was in command of the squad. "I'll take this boy down to the corner and we'll phone the Department of Justice and check up on his story."

While the police detail spread out to comb the street, the sergeant and Bob walked back to the police car.

"It will go hard on you, kid, if you're trying to pull anything on us," warned the sergeant.

"Don't worry about that," Bob reassured him. "Just let me get to a telephone where I can get in touch with Waldo Edgar."

They walked to the corner and then turned to their right. Half way down the next block there was a small drug store and they found a pay telephone there. Bob entered the booth while the sergeant, a blocky, dark-haired man of about 40, stuck his foot in the door so that it would remain open and he could hear the conversation.

"Hand me your papers," he told Bob, and the young federal agent handed over the small leather case which he carried in an inner pocket.

Bob's fingers skimmed the pages of the telephone directory until he found the desired number. Dropping a nickel in the phone, he dialed for the Department of Justice. When an operator answered, he gave his message quickly and concisely.

"I'll give you Mr. Edgar at once," promised the operator.

It was only a few seconds later when Bob heard the voice of the chief of the division of investigation of the Department of Justice. It was a rich full voice, that once heard would never be forgotten. Bob identified himself quickly and then in rapid, sentences told what had happened.

"Your uncle had the paper the last you saw of him?" asked the federal chief.

"Yes," replied Bob. "He was attempting to reach the far end of the street and escape while I attracted the attention of the men trying to capture him. But I was knocked out and I don't know what happened. When the police arrived the street was deserted and the bullet-proof sedan was missing."

"We'll spread an alarm at once," said Edgar. "See that you are released at once by the police. Then come here at once."

Bob turned to the sergeant.

"Satisfied about my identity?" he asked.

"You're okay," grinned the sergeant, handing back the leather case, which Bob slipped into his coat.

"I'll be over at once," he promised the federal chief.

He stepped out of the booth and started to hasten toward the door, but a question from the sergeant detained him.

"Can you give us a description of that car? We'll have it broadcast over the police radio and also on the teletype circuit. Some of our men may pick up the machine and the sooner we can get a report the better chance we'll have of finding your uncle."

Bob's description of the car was meager. He wasn't even sure of the make, but it had looked like a large Romney sedan.

"The windshield is shattered and there ought to be a number of bullet marks on the body," he said. "I guess that will be the best way to identify it."

"We'll shut down on every road out of the city. They can't get away," promised the sergeant, as he stepped back into the booth to telephone the description to police headquarters.

But Bob had his own doubts as to whether the police would be able to apprehend the car. Too much time had elapsed. Even now the big machine might be speeding out of the city.

It was then that Bob disobeyed his orders from the federal chief. Instead of summoning a taxi, he hastened back to the street where the attack had taken place. He wanted to be sure that his uncle had not been wounded and left there.

When he arrived the police squad had completed its search.

"Find anyone?" asked Bob anxiously.

"Not even a good ghost," grumbled one of the officers. "Say, that taxi's a wreck."

But Bob had no time to waste in talk over a damaged taxi. He half ran and half walked to the nearest thoroughfare where he flagged a taxi and ordered the driver to take him to the Department of Justice building.

On the way over, Bob reviewed the events of the night. With the disappearance of his uncle the case had deepened and he felt as though he was drifting in a sea of puzzling problems.

On reaching the Department of Justice building, Bob went directly to the upper floor where the federal chief's office was located. An agent, evidently watching for him, escorted him into the inner office and Bob's eyes widened as he saw Condon Adams and Tully Ross seated beside Waldo Edgar's desk.

The federal chief rose as Bob came in.

"Have a chair, Bob. We want to hear in detail everything that went on tonight. Now that your uncle has disappeared, you'll have to work with Adams and Ross here on the case. I'm counting on you for a lot of good work."

CHAPTER XXIV

A SOLITARY HAND

★

Bob, as he eased his weary body into a chair, looked at Condon Adams and Tully Ross. Both of them looked tired and worn and their faces reflected the strain they had been under since the escape of the prisoner from the police station.

"Some more bungling, I expect," snapped Condon Adams. The words were harsh and uncalled for, and Bob's temper flared quickly.

"If it was bungling, it wasn't the first bit of it today," he shot back at the older federal agent.

Adams' face flushed. He started to reply, then thought better of it, and remained silent.

"I want to know everything in detail, Bob," said the federal chief. "Just tell me all that happened this evening."

"We were eating dinner," said Bob, "when I happened to put my hand in my coat pocket and

I felt a paper in there. When I pulled it out and discovered what it was, I was dumfounded."

"Dumb-bell!" The word was whispered, but everyone in the room heard it and Bob whirled toward Tully.

"Another crack like that out of you and I'll take you all apart," he flared.

"Calm down, boys," said Waldo Edgar. "We've got to get facts and get them at once. A man's life may be hanging in the balance. Go on Bob."

Bob went on to describe the start of their trip to the Department of Justice building.

"We saw a car following us, but we were holding our own until we turned into a street where there was a lot of repair work going on. Our taxi driver tried to get through, but the cab became stalled and he took to his heels."

Bob paused a moment. The recent action in the street was so vivid that it was hard to describe.

"Uncle Merritt and I decided it would be better to try to make it alone and we parted just as these gunmen unloaded. I managed to crawl back to their car and when they started shooting at Uncle Merritt I took their car and rammed it down the street in an effort to attract their attention and give him a chance to escape."

"Is there any chance that he got away?" asked the federal chief, leaning forward anxiously in his chair.

Bob shook his head.

"The last thing I remember was a single shot and then someone cried, 'We've got him.' Then someone slugged me and I didn't regain consciousness until the police arrived. They haven't found a trace of him."

"I was afraid that was the case," said the federal chief. "We've swung a tight cordon around the entire city and I'm even having the airports checked. We won't overlook a single angle. Something will turn up before morning."

The telephone buzzed and the federal chief, seized it eagerly, but his face fell as some routine message came over the wire.

When he had completed the conversation, he turned toward Condon Adams.

"Now that Merritt Hughes is off the case, you'll be in direct charge of finding him and recovering that paper. I'm assigning Bob to give you some help wherever you need it."

Adams showed his displeasure, but he was careful not to make it too obvious to Waldo Edgar.

"Thanks," he grunted. "I may need the kid for some leg work, but he always seems to be getting into trouble." It was biting sarcasm, but Bob chose to ignore it.

"This latest development," went on the federal chief, "puts us right back where we were after we thought the paper had vanished from the office, while in reality it was in Bob's pocket. The one prisoner who could have given us some information slipped out of our hands and one of my best agents has been abducted. That means whoever is after this information is both desperate and daring."

The federal chief looked at Bob, whose face was still flushed from the recent fight in the street.

"Got a gun, Bob?"

"I've a .32."

Waldo Edgar shook his head.

"That's not heavy enough," he summoned an assistant, who returned shortly with a stubby but serviceable gun and two clips of cartridges.

"This is a new gun with which we are equipping our agents," explained Edgar. "It's a .45 and when you hit anything with that, you stop it, even if it is a freight train. You can't afford to go rummaging around Washington at night without ample protection while you're on this case."

"So far I've been able to make pretty good use of my fists," grinned Bob, "but this may come in handy in a pinch."

"Any orders for Bob tonight?" asked Edgar, directing his question at Condon Adams.

"I won't need him," was the tart reply. "He might as well go home and get some sleep."

"I may get a little sleep, but I'm not going home," replied Bob. "That's too popular with certain unpleasant people. You can find me at a hotel and I'll probably change my address every night."

He named a·small hotel which was near his own room.

"That's a good idea," said Waldo Edgar, "but be sure to keep us informed every time you shift to a new address. We'll let you know the minute we get any information on your uncle. Now you'd better get home and get some sleep."

Bob admitted that he was mighty tired, but he was far from sleepy for his mind was still spinning in circles.

When he left the office Condon Adams and Tully Ross stepped out into the hall with him and they descended to the main floor in the same elevator. Bob could feel the cold wave of animosity which engulfed the others and he knew that though they would make every effort to recover the radio secret, they probably would not overtax their energies in finding his uncle.

As they walked toward the main door, Condon Adams spoke.

"We'll call on you when we need help, but this thing is going to be easy. Too bad your uncle muffed it this afternoon."

Bob wheeled and faced him squarely.

"Let's have an understanding right now. In the first place, my uncle didn't muff anything. I'd like to have seen you do any better than he did when three gunmen were shooting at you in a dark street and the only escape was at an end where there was a brilliant street light. Now as far as getting things in a mess, it seems to me that you did a perfect job when you let that prisoner, the one man who could have supplied valuable information, take your gun away from you in the police station this afternoon. That makes you out to be quite a chump and I've always thought you were."

Bob was surprised at his own words and his own boldness, but he saw a look something like apprehension in Condon Adams' eyes.

"You don't like my uncle; you never have. You've always been jealous of his brains and his ability. Your nephew doesn't like me. Well, that goes for me, too. I don't think you'll make any effort to find my uncle. If you can recover that paper, well and good—that's your first thought. But I'm serving notice on you right now that I'm going to find him and I'm going to recover that paper. And I'll do it without any help from either one of you. So here's a tip. I'm tired and I'm mad and I don't like you. Right now I can think of nothing I'd like to do better than give each of you a biff on the nose and if you open your mouths again about my uncle, I'll do just that thing. Good night."

Bob's words had so amazed both Adams and

his nephew that they were speechless and the young federal agent turned and stepped through the main doorway.

Tully Ross, angry words crowding to his lips, started to follow Bob, but the firm hands of Condon Adams stopped him.

"Keep your head, Tully," he warned. "The boy's mad clear through and he'd do just what he said—clean up on both of us. Maybe we've got it coming, though. We baited him too much. But we're going to find that missing radio document."

The same resolution was in Bob's heart as he stepped down the avenue, but in addition was the grim determination that he would find his uncle.

CHAPTER XXV

THE FIRST CLUE

★

THE coolness of the fall night helped to clear the mad whirl of Bob's fatigued mind and he mulled over the things that had happened as he walked down the avenue.

For nearly 24 hours the missing paper had been in his possession, which accounted for the attempt to kidnap him. But how had it leaked that the paper had been sent over to the archives division for filing—who had known that he would be alone that night?

Bob felt that knowing the answer to this question, he would have something on which to base his further investigation.

Then there was the disappearance of his uncle that night. Bob knew that both the radio document and the federal agent were in the hands of ruthless and relentless men. From what his uncle had told him before, the radio secret was worth a huge amount to almost every foreign power and he dared not guess what country might be interested in obtaining its possession through such means as had been employed.

Bob's walk took him to the archives building and he automatically turned in and went up to the office where he worked.

The guard on duty on that floor was a familiar one, and Bob spoke to him briefly.

"Anything unusual tonight?" he asked.

"Not a thing," was the quick and honest reply.

Bob walked down the corridor, unlocked the door of the office, switched on the lights, and stepped inside.

The room appeared to be just as he had left it in the afternoon and Bob sat down at his desk. It was quiet here and he would have an opportunity to think out some of his problems.

But he found himself too tired even for that. His head was heavy and he drowsed at his desk. Half an hour passed and Bob fell into a sound slumber. For an hour he slept at his desk until the tapping of the guard at the door aroused him.

Bob opened the door in response to the summons.

"Thought something might have happened to you," said the guard, half apologetically.

"Something did," smiled Bob. "I went sound asleep. I'd better get out of here and get to bed."

While the guard looked on, Bob turned off the lights, locked the room and started toward the elevator.

The guard halted him a few paces down the hall.

"Sorry, Mr. Houston, but I'll have to search you. There's a new rule that anyone working on this floor out of hours must be searched."

Bob was half inclined to be angry, but he realized the soundness of this rule, especially after what had just taken place. He quietly submitted to a careful search of his clothing by the guard.

"You know your job," said Bob when the search was over.

"I used to be a store detective," replied the other, with not a little pride in his voice, "and if I do say it myself, I was one of the best in Washington."

It was only a few blocks to the hotel at which Bob had decided to take up temporary quarters, and he walked the short distance at a brisk pace.

He registered, asking for a quiet, inside room, but the clerk looked dubious when Bob informed him he had no baggage, but would arrange to have his clothes sent down in the morning.

"You'll have to pay in advance," he said.

Bob delved into his pockets in search of money and to his embarrassment found that he had less than a dollar.

The clerk appeared skeptical. It was late and after the fight in the street Bob's clothes were in none too good condition.

"Perhaps you'd better try another hotel," he suggested.

By that time Bob longed for nothing more than a comfortable bed and a few hours of sleep and his feet were heavy. They wouldn't have carried him another block.

Reaching inside his coat he pulled out the billfold and drew out the identification badge which had been given to him by the federal chief.

"I guess this will identify me, even though I'm temporarily short of funds," said Bob. "Now I want that room and I don't want to be disturbed unless there is something really important. Understand?"

The clerk stared at the identification card and his whole manner changed into one of the utmost courtesy. In less than ten minutes Bob was in bed, to drop into a sleep that was to be disturbed hours later by the strident ringing of the telephone on the stand beside his bed.

It was broad daylight when Bob rubbed the sleep from his eyes and answered the telephone.

"Yes, this is Bob Houston speaking," he said.

The words which came over the wire caught and held his attention.

"Yes, I understand. Of course, come right over. I'll be dressed and ready to go over the entire affair."

Bob hung up the receiver, reached the bathroom in one long jump, and in another had the shower on and was under it.

After a brisk shower, he rubbed his body down thoroughly, feeling ready for what he knew was to be a busy day. The caller was Lieut. Frederick Gibbons of the intelligence unit of the War Department, who had been assigned to help on the case. He had promised Bob information of vital importance and almost before Bob had finished dressing there was a knock.

When Bob opened the door a trim, soldierly figure was standing in the hall.

"Lieutenant Gibbons?" asked Bob.

"Right. I take it you're Bob Houston?"

Bob nodded.

"How about breakfast?" asked the intelligence officer.

"I'm ready now and hungry," grinned Bob.

"Then we'll eat and talk. The coffee shop down stairs is excellent."

After they had placed their orders for breakfast, Lieutenant Gibbons leaned toward Bob.

"How long have you been asleep?" he asked.

"It must have been nearly three o'clock before I went to bed here," was the reply.

"Then a lot of things have happened since you dropped out of this thing."

"Has my uncle been found?" asked Bob anxiously.

"I'm sorry, but he hasn't. However, we've turned up some clues that may prove mighty interesting. The car in which he was abducted has been found."

"Where?" The question was sharp and anxious.

"Down near the tidal basin."

"Was there any trace of him?"

"There was a stain or two on the rear cushions of the car, but nothing serious, so if he was wounded last night, I don't think we need to worry about that."

"But the tidal basin? Does that mean——?"

Though Bob left the question unfinished, the lieutenant guessed what he feared and was quick to ease his mind.

"I'm sure your uncle is still a captive. We've learned that sometime late in the night a high-speed motor boat dashed out of the basin and down the Potomac. It was a strange boat that came up the river early in the evening. We've a fairly good description of the craft and may be able to trace it down. Now our first mission is to locate your uncle and recover that paper."

Bob liked the manner in which Lieutenant Gibbons spoke. The intelligence officer looked keen and alive to everything. He was a little taller than Bob and slender with a slenderness that was wiry. His eyes were a sparkling brown and there was an upward twist to his lips that Bob liked.

"Have you heard whether Condon Adams and Tully Ross have turned up anything?" asked Bob.

A frown marred the lieutenant's forehead.

"They've been busy," he said. "As a matter of fact, they've caused the arrest of Arthur Jacobs. They found some rather suspicious looking things at his apartment, including some half burned scraps of paper in a fireplace in which someone was offering Jacobs $5,000 for information on the radio secrets."

"Does it look like a real lead?" Bob was anxious.

"It may, but I hate to believe it. Jacobs is a foreigner and he has a brother who only recently escaped from a midwestern prison and who has made a bad record."

"Does his description tally with that of the fellow who escaped from jail?"

"That's just it. There is a real resemblance and Condon Adams says he is certain that Jacobs' brother, Fritz, is the man who escaped from him."

"Maybe Adams is too anxious to build up a case," said Bob.

"That's true, but the facts are starting to click and it looks like the Jacobs brothers are going to be in for some unpleasant hours. Arthur is down at the central station now."

"But it doesn't seem possible. I've known him for a long time; he didn't seem like the kind who would get involved in anything like this."

"That's just when you lose your way," he said. "Don't take anything for granted. If you want to succeed in intelligence work you have to put a question mark around everyone."

Chapter XXVI

A BREAK FOR BOB

★

BREAKFAST at an end, they left the hotel and the intelligence officer hailed a taxicab.

"We'll go down and listen in on this grilling," he said.

Bob didn't relish seeing Arthur Jacobs, his filing chief, under the barrage of questions he knew Condon Adams would hurl at the little man, but he steeled his nerves for he knew that in his new work he must be willing and prepared to face many an ordeal.

They found a small group in a plain room. There was none of the pictured "third degree" methods.

Arthur Jacobs looked worried and tired. He sat behind a table, a pitcher and glass of water within easy reach. Lounging across the table from him was Adams, his fingers drumming incessantly on the table. At another table at one side sat a stenographer and Tully Ross was sitting in a chair tilted back against the wall.

Just after Bob and the intelligence officer arrived, Waldo Edgar looked in.

"Any results?" he asked.

"Not so far," grunted Condon Adams, "but this fellow has a story to tell and he's going to break pretty soon."

A look of desperation flickered for a moment in Arthur Jacobs' eyes and he turned toward Bob.

"Hello, Mr. Jacobs," said Bob. "I didn't think I'd ever see you here."

There was just a trace of a smile around the filing chief's lips when he replied.

"I never thought I would be here, Bob. Who's in charge of the office with both of us away?"

"I don't know, but I'll find out if you like."

"I would," said the filing chief simply and Bob stepped into an adjoining office and telephoned the archives division, where he was informed that a senior clerk from another office had taken over the duties temporarily.

When Bob stepped back into the larger room, Jacobs was sweating freely.

"Everything's all right at the office," volunteered Bob, who felt sorry for the little man. "Bondurance, from the next office, is taking charge and they're getting along all right. Of course they miss you."

"I'm afraid they won't get those papers back in the proper order. It's an awful mess."

Bob agreed that it was and he couldn't make himself feel that Arthur Jacobs, so obviously worried about the routine at the office, could be guilty of anything very bad.

"Come on, now Jacobs," broke in the heavy voice of Condon Adams. "Quit this stalling and get down to business. How much did you get for selling out this secret?"

"But I tell you I didn't get anything," replied the filing chief, spreading his hands out on the table in a dramatic denial. "How many times must I tell you this?"

"Until you tell me the truth and admit that you were paid to sell information on a government secret."

"Oh, go away; quit bothering me," cried the man behind the table.

He stood up and pointed at Adams.

"Get out! Get out! Leave Bob here; I'll talk to him; I can trust him!"

Condon Adams half rose in utter surprise at the force of Jacobs' words. Then he dropped back into his chair and a look of sullen resentment swept over his face.

"You'll tell me, or no one," he growled.

But from the back of the room, where he had stepped in unnoticed, Waldo Edgar spoke quietly.

"Let Jacobs talk in his own way," he ruled. "The rest of us will step out while Bob talks with him."

The legs of the chair in which Tully Ross had been leaning back against the wall struck the floor with a thud and Tully started to protest, but his uncle, realizing the futility, waved him into silence.

Lieutenant Gibbons grinned at Bob as the others left the room. He was the last to step out and he closed the door carefully behind him.

When they were alone a tremendous burden seemed to lift from the shoulders of the filing chief.

"I've got to talk," he told Bob, in a voice so low that it would have been impossible for anyone at the door to hear. "But I had to talk with someone I could trust."

He paused for a moment.

"Your uncle is missing?"

"He was kidnaped last night," replied Bob. "There were three in the gang and they got him and the radio paper which was stolen from our file."

Arthur Jacobs nodded sorrowfully.

"I'm sorry about that, Bob, for he is in great danger then. I'll tell my story as quickly as I can; then you must act without loss of time."

Chapter XXVII

ACTION AHEAD

★

Arthur Jacobs wiped the perspiration from his forehead and then reached for the glass of water. He drained it at one gulp and leaned back in his chair, an air of relief on his face.

Bob, tense, waited for him to speak. When the words finally came they rushed out in a torrent and Bob heard a story that wrenched at his own heart.

"It's been terrible, Bob, terrible. I've got to tell you the whole story. When Fritz escaped from prison he made his way east and I had letters from him. He needed money; he had always needed money as far as that was concerned. When I sent word that I had none to spare, he started threatening me. Then he fell in with bad company and the first thing I knew he was here in Washington."

The filing chief paused a moment and wiped his forehead again for the perspiration was running freely.

"Fritz came to my apartment and demanded money, but I actually didn't have it. He went away for a while, and then came again later. It was on this visit last week that I got some inkling of what was in his mind. He started hinting around about the secrets which passed through my hands for filing and for safe-guarding. After an hour or so he came out in the open and made me a proposition. He knew where he could sell the secret of this new radio-propelled and guided plane if I could get my hands on the war department papers."

The filing chief stopped to pour out another glass of water.

"Go on," urged Bob, who was desperately anxious to learn the full story and then resume the hunt for his uncle.

"Fritz offered me $5,000 for my share if I would only tell him when the papers reached the office. He said that was all they needed to know. I could have used the $5,000, but I told him I wouldn't do such a thing. Then a couple of days later I got a letter from him. It was mailed somewhere over in Maryland and he repeated his offer and threatened me with exposing an old family scandal."

"That was the letter Condon Adams found," exclaimed Bob, and the filing chief nodded.

"I was careless about that. I tossed it in the fireplace, but didn't make sure that it had been consumed."

"But did you supply your brother with the necessary information?" asked Bob, pressing hard for more concrete information.

Arthur Jacobs lowered his head.

"Fritz came back the other night. He was in a terrible rage. He had promised to get this information from me, and had failed. You'll never know the fear I've always had of Fritz. He was bigger, older and he always bullied me. He threatened to beat me to death and I finally told him what he wanted to know."

Bob saw tears welling into the chief clerk's eyes and he turned his own face away, for it had not been easy to hear this confession. When the young federal agent finally looked back, Arthur Jacobs was composed and calm once more.

"When did you give him this information?"

"It was the night before you caught Fritz in the office," replied Jacobs.

"Have you seen him since then?"

"Yes, he came to my apartment after his escape and I sheltered him for a few hours. I didn't want to, but he was armed and forced me to do it. That's all I know about it."

"Don't you know who's behind Fritz? Who is supplying him with the money?"

Arthur Jacobs shook his head.

"I didn't even see any money," he said bitterly. "Fritz said that would come later after this thing had been forgotten."

Bob felt sorry for the little man, for he knew now that Jacobs had been the unwilling dupe of an older and bullying brother.

There was one bit of information Bob must have, one thing that was vital.

"Did you save the envelope in which the letter Fritz sent you from Maryland was mailed?" he asked.

Jacobs ran his fingers through his thinning hair.

"I can't remember."

"Did you toss it in the fireplace?"

"No, I don't think so. I probably dropped it in the wastebasket. The maid cleans my apartment each day."

"Then where would this type of rubbish go?"

"Down to the janitor, who would burn it in the incinerator."

Bob reached for the telephone on the other table.

"Give me the number of your apartment house," he urged, and Jacobs supplied the needed information.

The building superintendent answered and Bob's words fairly tumbled over the wire.

"This is Bob Houston, a federal agent speaking," he said. "Get hold of your janitor at once. Don't allow him to burn any more waste paper or refuse of any type from the floor on which Arthur Jacobs lives. I'll be there within half an hour to check up on you."

The building superintendent was inclined to argue, but Bob cut him short.

"This is no time for words," he said. "Do as you're told or I'll file a charge against you for interfering with the work of a federal officer."

Actually Bob didn't know whether he had

that power or not, but the words sounded well and the threat did what was intended—the superintendent changed his tone and agreed to halt the burning of any more wastepaper or refuse.

Bob turned back from the telephone and Jacobs looked at him with a brighter face.

"I don't know what's going to happen to me," he said, "but I feel better for having told you."

"I'll help you all I can," promised Bob heartily, turning to call for Lieutenant Gibbons.

The intelligence officer opened the door almost instantly and Condon Adams and Tully Ross crowded in close behind him.

"Well, can you solve the mystery for us now?" asked Adams, his voice heavy with sarcasm.

"I think so," replied Bob.

"Let's have it, then."

"Hardly. Solve it in your own way. Remember that I'm working with my uncle on this case. You have the invaluable help of Tully."

"That's enough of smart cracks like that," replied Adams, his face flushing a little. "I want to know what Jacobs said."

"I'm making my report direct to Mr. Edgar. You'll have to get it from him."

With that Bob left the room and went directly to the office of the federal chief, Lieutenant Gibbons trailing at his heels.

Waldo Edgar listened intently while Bob recounted what Jacobs had told him.

"I rather sensed what his story would be," mused the chief investigator.

"Don't you believe it?" asked Bob.

"Yes, every word of it. Just another case of an older and bullying brother taking advantage of a weaker one. It looks like Jacobs has supplied us with the key information we have been groping for. Good work, Bob."

"I'm afraid I don't deserve any congratulations. Adams turned up Jacobs as a suspect."

"True enough, but Jacobs would never have talked for Adams or any of the rest of us. The important thing is that he did talk to you. Now what are you planning?"

Bob told of the letter from Maryland and of his orders to the building superintendent.

"The postmark on that letter should give us a clue to where the gang took my uncle," he said. "There isn't much chance of finding it, but it's worth the time and effort."

Waldo Edgar's eyes brightened.

"You're going to do, my boy. It's things like that that count. You never can tell when even the tiniest slip of paper is going to give you the key to the case you're working on."

The chief agent turned to Lieutenant Gibbons.

"You're staying on the case with Bob?" he asked.

"I'm going to try and keep up with him," smiled the intelligence officer.

"Splendid. Then we'll expect your uncle and the missing radio paper within the next twenty-four hours, Bob."

Chapter XXVIII

WASTE PAPER

★

THERE was a real feeling of hope in Bob's heart as he stepped out of the Department of Justice building with Lieutenant Gibbons at his side.

"Things are going to move fast from now on," predicted the lieutenant. "By the way, Bob, aren't you a little young to be a federal agent?"

"I'm not a full-fledged agent," explained Bob. "When my uncle was assigned to this case and it looked like some valuable information might be gained by an inside man in our office, I was delegated to help him and given papers as a provisional agent. If I make good on this case I may get into the service permanently, even though I'm a little young."

"I think you're going in with a rush and I know you're going to make good even though Edgar gave you a pretty short time when he said you'd have the case solved within twenty-four hours."

"That's what scares me," confessed Bob, "but I've got to find my uncle. Once he's safe I'll start worrying about the radio secret."

"When you find him you'll recover the radio secret," predicted the intelligence officer.

Fifteen minutes of fast driving in a taxi took them to the apartment where Arthur Jacobs resided.

The building superintendent, curious and somewhat worried over Bob's telephoned orders, was waiting at the door to meet them.

Bob identified himself and the superintendent admitted them to the building, taking them into the basement where an incinerator bulked in the background. Beside it were a number of bales of paper.

"We've been baling and selling the waste paper," he explained, "but I can't tell you in what bale the paper from the fourth floor, where Jacobs lives, can be found. It's a good thing you phoned. We were going to have this trucked out sometime during the day."

Bob looked at the bales and a feeling of dismay crept into his heart. All he wanted was one envelope—a small slip of paper—yet there were literally hundreds of pieces of paper in each one of the bales. He turned to Lieutenant Gibbons. The intelligence officer grinned.

"Looks like we're in for it. Better get off your coat, Bob, and we'll start on the first bale."

"You mean you want to open up all those bales?" demanded the building superintendent.

"That's right," nodded the intelligence officer. "We not only want to, but we're going to do it. Get some snippers and cut through the wires on this bale." He indicated the huge stack of paper nearest him.

The superintendent snapped on additional lights and grudgingly cut the wires on the first bale while Bob took off his coat.

"Save every envelope with a Maryland postmark on it," he said.

It looked like an endless task, but Bob and the lieutenant, squatting on their heels, started through the pile of paper.

The building superintendent, after watching them for several minutes, joined in the hunt.

At the end of half an hour they had found

four letters with Maryland postmarks on them, but none of them addressed to Arthur Jacobs.

"We've got to have more help," decided the intelligence officer when an hour had slipped away and they had gone through only one bale. He went to a telephone and called the department of justice, with the result that within half an hour six other agents were on the job, delving through the growing pile of papers.

By noon they had examined every scrap of paper from five bales and their arms and backs were aching sharply.

"I'm dizzy," confessed the intelligence officer when they finally stopped for lunch. Leaving one of the agents to guard the bales in the basement, the others went to a nearby restaurant. Lunch was eaten quickly and with a minimum of talk, for every one of them knew that perhaps a man's life hinged on the quickness with which they could find the tell-tale envelope.

They carried a tray of lunch back to the agent who had been left on guard and plunged once more into the mountainous task which still faced them.

The early hours of the afternoon slipped away.

Bale after bale of paper was scanned with care and Bob felt his hopes sinking.

Another bale was finished and one more pulled down and clipped open. He knelt down again and picked up a handful of waste paper. An envelope drew his attention, but it was for another resident on the floor on which the filing chief lived.

Lieutenant Gibbons, whose lanky form was almost doubled in a knot from the hours of bending down and looking at slips of paper, suddenly straightened up with a triumphant cry.

"Here's the letter!" he cried, waving a badly torn envelope.

The federal men, dropping the paper they had been sorting, rushed to his side.

Bob was the first to see the postmark on the envelope. It was marked from Rubio, Maryland, and was addressed to Arthur Jacobs.

The handwriting on the envelope was large and heavy and the pen which had been used was none too good for it had dropped ink in two places on the envelope.

Bob felt his heart leap. This was the clue they had sought for so many weary, back-breaking hours in the litter of paper in the basement.

"How far is it to Rubio?" Bob asked the intelligence officer.

"I'm not sure that I even know what part of Maryland it's in, but I believe if we go by plane, we should be there in an hour."

"Then we'll go by plane," decided Bob.

Just how he could obtain a plane was a question he couldn't have answered at the moment, but he was determined to make the trip with the least possible loss of time for he felt that either in Rubio or near it he would find the solution to the mystery.

CHAPTER XXIX

INTO THE AIR

★

Bob and Lieutenant Gibbons left the other federal agents at the apartment building to help the superintendent clean up the litter of paper they had strewn about the basement while they hastened back to the Department of Justice building.

Waldo Edgar himself was waiting for their report and he smiled contentedly when he heard it.

"You're on the right track, Bob. Follow it hard and don't let a single trick get away from you. How are you going to Rubio?"

Bob turned to a wall map which showed the entire state of Maryland. As Lieutenant Gibbons had surmised, Rubio was on the east shore, a tiny dot of a town, well isolated from any of the other shore villages.

"That's a desolate stretch," said the chief. "You may need help in rounding up this gang."

"We'll try it alone," said Bob. "If we find them, we can send in a call for assistance. Can you arrange for us to fly there?"

The chief of the division of investigation looked at his watch. It was just three o'clock.

"A plane will be ready in half an hour at Antacostia," he said. "Make sure that you are well armed and don't take unnecessary risks. Understand?"

"Yes, sir," replied Bob.

"Then start for Antacostia at once. You're going, too, lieutenant?"

"I wouldn't miss this," replied the intelligence officer. "Besides, we have a considerable stake in this game."

"Splendid. But don't let Bob take any needless risks. I'm counting on his developing into one of my aces one of these days."

Bob's temperature rose about three degrees and he looked at the federal chief to see if he was joking, but Waldo Edgar was serious.

"Looks to me like you're making headway rapidly," said Lieutenant Gibbons as they left the Department of Justice building. "You carrying a gun?" he asked.

Bob patted his coat pocket.

"I've got a special .45 with an extra clip of cartridges. That ought to be enough for a trip like this."

"Let's hope so," said the intelligence officer.

When they reached Antacostia, a cabin plane, a navy ship, was out on the ramp waiting for them. It was an amphibian and while they were paying the driver of their cab, the pilot started the motor with a roar that shook the ground.

An officer ran toward them.

"Which one of you is Bob Houston?" he asked.

Bob stepped forward.

"You're wanted on the phone at once," he said.

"Step on it, Bob. We're ready to go," warned Lieutenant Gibbons.

Bob ran toward the administration building and a clerk there handed him a telephone.

Bob recognized instantly the voice of the chief of the bureau of investigation. Waldo Edgar, usually so calm, was deeply moved.

"Bob, get to Rubio with all possible speed. We've just had reports that an unknown yet tremendously powerful radio station has just

come on the air. The department of commerce
has had radio direction finders on it for the last
ten minutes and they report that the station must
be on the east shore of Maryland, probably near
Rubio. They're throwing on extra power on
their experimental station here to gum up the
sending from this unknown outfit. I'm afraid
they're trying to get the secret of the radio-
controlled plane out of the country in this way."

"We're all ready to go. The plane's on the
ramp now with the motor on."

"Then hurry. Let me know the minute you
land at Rubio and I can send more information.
I'm starting agents out of Baltimore by motor
and I'll send another plane with men within the
hour. Good luck."

Bob turned and raced toward the waiting plane.

"What news?" asked Lieutenant Gibbons.

"Tell you when we're in the air," replied Bob.

They climbed into the cabin and were no
sooner seated than the ship started rolling across
the field.

Almost before they knew it the ground was
dropping away and they were headed for the
east shore of Maryland.

CHAPTER XXX

ON THE EAST SHORE

★

THE air that fall afternoon was clear and the entire panorama of the city of Washington spread out below them. But Bob's thoughts were not on the beauties of the afternoon or of the flight. His mind was centered far ahead on the east shore village of Rubio and what he might learn there.

The cabin was well insulated, so Bob and Lieutenant Gibbons could converse in comparative ease.

"What did Edgar have to say?" asked the intelligence officer.

"He's afraid the gang is trying to get the secret radio information out of the country by using an unlicensed station which has just started broadcasting from somewhere along the east shore of Maryland."

Lieutenant Gibbons whistled.

"What's he doing about it?"

"Federal agents are being sent from Baltimore by motor and another plane is to follow us within a few minutes. The department of commerce believes the station is near Rubio and they're trying to gum up the broadcast as much as possible. Oh, it all clicks beautifully. My uncle was taken down the river in a fast boat and landed somewhere near Rubio. He had the paper they desired and now they are trying to send the information someplace in Europe by using this powerful but unlicensed radio."

"Sounds logical," agreed the lieutenant. "Looks like we're going to have some busy hours ahead of us. Made any plans yet?"

Bob shook his head.

"I haven't thought any beyond getting to Rubio as fast as we can and trying to learn there whether a boat like the one which slipped out of the tidal basin last night has been sighted there."

"Think we can swing it alone or are you going to wait for the other agents to catch up with us?"

There was no hesitation in Bob's reply.

"We're going on as rapidly as we can. Every

minute counts now. We may run straight into a whole kettle of trouble, but we'll have to handle it in some fashion."

They lapsed into silence as the sturdy amphibian sped out over Chesapeake Bay. Fishing boats could be seen below and several freighters, bound for Baltimore, churned up a white wake in the blue of the bay. It was indeed a calm and peaceful afternoon but Bob's mind was anything but peaceful or calm.

Then they were over Maryland and a few minutes later the uneven line of the east shore was visible.

The pilot, in his cockpit up ahead, was scanning the ground intently. The ship veered a little to the right and they circled over a sprawling village before which a broad, sandy beach broke the gentle swell of the Atlantic. Half a mile from the village proper was a sheltered cove with a score of small fishing wharfs. It was toward this that the pilot of the amphibian nosed his craft.

As they swung over the cove Bob could see the upturned faces of fishermen as they stared at the unexpected visitor. Bob looked at the boats in the cove with extreme care, but none of them were unusual and none appeared capable of great speed.

The amphibian smacked the water and spray flew out on both sides as they slowed down and taxied in toward the shore. The pilot cut the engine when they were near a low wharf and dropped a light anchor.

A friendly fisherman put out in a dory and pulled alongside the plane.

"Any trouble?" he asked.

"Not yet," replied Lieutenant Gibbons, "but we're looking for a black speed boat. It's been described as about 30 feet long and capable of 40 miles an hour. It's a cabin boat with an antennae above the cabin. Ever seen anything like it around here?"

Bob, watching the fisherman closely, thought he detected a slight narrowing of the other's eyes, but he knew that the men of the east shore were by nature extremely cautious.

"Don't know as I've seen just that boat," replied the fisherman, "but there's a good many crafts slip around the coves here."

"This boat would have come in this morning."

"Better climb in.   We'll ask some of the other boys."

Bob and the intelligence officer seated themselves in the dory and were quickly put ashore, where a little group gathered about them.

The man who had brought them ashore acted as spokesman.

"These fellows are looking for a speedboat that might have come around here this morning. Anybody seen anything of such a craft?"

There was no immediate reply and Bob could see doubt as to the wisdom of answering the question in the eyes of a number of the men.   It was then that he decided to tell them the importance of their visit.

He drew out his billfold and handed the nearest man his identification card.

"We're federal officers," he explained, "and we're looking for a man who was kidnaped last night in Washington in a speedboat and brought somewhere near Rubio. If you can give us any information it may save a man's life."

The entire attitude of the group changed and a young man who had been in the background stepped forward.

"I saw such a boat just about mid-forenoon," he said. "It was coming up from the south, and coming fast, maybe forty an hour, but I didn't see it put in any place."

A radio in one of the fishing shacks screeched as though in agony and the owner of the set hurried away to tune it down.

"Somebody ought to break that thing up; it's been doing that all afternoon," grunted another fisherman.

"Did it work all right before?" asked Bob.

"Sure. But this afternoon something went wrong and we can't get anything."

Bob knew then that the end of the trail was nearing.

"Tell me this: Are there any old estates near here which have been recently occupied?"

The owner of the radio, who had shut it off, rejoined the group in time to hear Bob's question, and it was he who replied.

"There's the old Haskins place about five miles up the shore," he said. "Someone's been around there for the last month or so. I went up one day to try and sell some provisions, but they ordered me off."

"Could this speedboat have been bound for the Haskins place?" asked Bob, aiming his question at the young fisherman who had told him about the boat.

"Sure, it was going up the shore. But I've never seen that boat around here before."

Bob turned to Lieutenant Gibbons.

"Looks to me like the Haskins place is our goal. Let's reconnoiter it in the plane."

"The sooner the better," agreed the intelligence officer.

Bob swung back to the fishermen.

"Federal agents are coming in here from Baltimore by car and from Washington by plane. If they arrive before we return, direct them to the Haskins place."

CHAPTER XXXI

THE CHASE ENDS

★

WITH its motor on full, the amphibian flashed across the cove and wheeled into the air. Bob felt that they were on the last leg of their hunt and he sensed a tenseness of his whole body that was unsettling. Lieutenant Gibbons realized how Bob felt and he leaned over and spoke to the young federal agent.

"Let your nerves loosen up a little and keep your head when we get on the ground. If we get in a jam, use your gun only as a last resort. Remember that help will be along soon."

The intelligence officer took out his own automatic and examined it, making sure that the firing mechanism was working perfectly. Bob did likewise and shifted the gun into his right hand coat pocket. He knew that with the gun there he could shoot through his pocket if necessary.

The village of Rubio dropped behind them and a desolate stretch of shore unfolded before their eyes.

Lieutenant Gibbons was the first to sight the Haskins place, a rambling old structure well out on a neck of land that projected into the Atlantic. He signalled to the pilot that this was their destination and the naval airman banked the amphibian gracefully.

The plane dropped low, flying not more than a hundred feet above the shore. The expansive old house, which had several long wings, was badly in need of paint, as were the outbuildings clustered to the rear. A long, low boathouse was built as a part of the run-down pier and one door was closed, but as the plane flashed by Bob caught a glimpse of a black motorboat and his heart leaped. He seized Lieutenant Gibbons' arm.

"I saw a boat in the shed!" cried Bob. "Let's get down as soon as possible."

But already the flyer was dropping the amphibian low. They spattered down on the water and their speed dropped off as they neared the old wharf.

Bob watched the house closely for some sign

of life. The windows, many of them broken, betrayed no movements. From all outward appearances the house had not been occupied in years.

The amphibian, now less than 50 yards from the beach, lost headway and drifted.

"Looks like some bad rocks ahead," said the pilot. "I don't dare get any closer. You'll have to swim if you want to land here unless I taxi out and down a ways. It looked better further down."

But Bob had no intention of wasting any more time.

"I'm going ashore," he told Lieutenant Gibbons. "You can stay here and see if anything happens."

Before the intelligence officer could protest, Bob eased himself out of the cabin and started swimming for shore. In a few yards he was able to touch bottom, but just as he straightened up there was a sharp puff from one of the lower windows of the old house and a bullet riccocheted along the water.

Bob, acting by instinct, ducked and started swimming under water. He should have been greatly alarmed, but instead he felt a strange exultation for the firing of that shot had told him what he wanted to know—he was at the end of the trail.

The young federal agent came up for air and as soon as his head appeared, three shots sounded in rapid succession, each fired from different windows in the house.

Two of the bullets went wide of their mark, but the third splashed water in Bob's eyes. Before he ducked again he heard Lieutenant Gibbons firing back and then another gun joined in the battle and Bob knew that the naval flyer had taken a hand in the party.

Swimming with a powerful stroke, Bob shot along under water. When he came up this time he was in the shelter of the boathouse. He was able to stand erect and he waved back to Lieutenant Gibbons. The firing from the house had suddenly ceased and Bob made his way alongside the squat, powerful speedboat.

He climbed into the craft and with several well aimed blows with the butt of his gun disabled the ignition apparatus. At least the kidnapers would not escape in the boat.

From some place behind the house the sound of an automobile exhaust roared out and Bob leaped to the door of the boathouse. A car wheeled around the far corner of the house and he saw three men inside, two in front and one in the rear. It was the first time Bob had ever fired a gun with a human being as a target, but he fired rapidly from the automatic and it seemed to him that a whole volley of bullets issued from the weapon in his hands. Then the gun was silent and before he could get the other clip from his pocket the car had disappeared.

Bob started running for the house, pausing only once when a cry from Lieutenant Gibbons caused him to turn his head. The intelligence officer was wading ashore and motioning for Bob to wait for him. But Bob had more pressing duties.

The front door of the house was half open and Bob charged through. The interior was dusty and unkempt, although there were some signs that an effort had been made to live in two of the front rooms.

Lieutenant Gibbons pounded up the front steps and burst into the hallway. He joined Bob and together they resumed the frantic search of the house. The first floor was combed, room for room and closet by closet, and it was not until they reached a shed at the back of the house that they found what they were seeking. There, laying on a roll of dirty bedding, was Merritt Hughes, bound, gagged and with a red welt along one side of his head.

Bob, a cry of joy at finding his uncle on his lips, bent down to untie the gag while Lieutenant Gibbons slashed at the rope which fastened the federal agent's wrists and ankles.

Together they helped Merritt Hughes to his feet. His tongue was badly swollen from the gag, but he managed to say a few words.

"Did they get away?" he asked slowly.

"Yes, but I don't think they'll get far. Agents are on their way from Baltimore and Washington," said Bob.

"How about their radio?"

"The department of commerce heard them come on the air and gummed up their broadcasts," replied Bob.

Lieutenant Gibbons, who had gone in search of water, returned with a tin cup and Merritt

Hughes drank it with relish, taking slow, deep draughts of the refreshing liquid.

Then he bathed his face and hands and felt much refreshed. He looked quizzically at Bob and the lieutenant.

"You fellows may catch pneumonia running around here in wet clothes," he warned.

"What happened to your head?" demanded the lieutenant.

"They creased me with a bullet during the scrap back in Washington last night," replied the federal agent grimly. "I want you to see their radio."

He led them to the top floor of the old house where one room had been fitted up for broad-casting purposes. Bob knew little about radio, but he could tell that a great deal of money had been expended here.

"Where's the aerial?" he asked.

"They used an underground antennae," replied his uncle.

Lieutenant Gibbons picked up a heavy chair which was in the room and deliberately smashed the delicate equipment.

"I guess that's the end of this station."

"But we haven't recovered the radio document," groaned Bob.

"I rather think we have," replied the lieutenant, pointing from a window to a cavalcade of cars which was approaching through a clearing.

CHAPTER XXXII

"FEDERAL AGENT"

★

THE scene that night in the office of the chief of the bureau of investigation was one that would remain stamped forever in Bob's memory.

Waldo Edgar was there. So was Bob's uncle and on the other side of the room were Tully Ross and Condon Adams and in the background Lieutenant Gibbons chuckled occasionally.

It was a brief session with Waldo Edgar doing most of the talking in that close, clipped manner of speech of his which inspired his own agents and instilled fear in the hearts of the men he was pursuing.

"The reports you have turned over to me to-night are highly gratifying," he said, "and I think we can call this case completed. While most of the honor of the final catch goes to Bob Houston, Condon Adams and Tully Ross deserve credit for uncovering that vital clue in the fireplace of Arthur Jacobs' apartment."

The federal chief shuffled through some papers on his desk.

"All of the men involved in the case have been apprehended, including Fritz Jacobs, who appeared to be the ringleader. Their radio station has been destroyed and they were unable to make use of the information which they had for nearly 24 hours. You may be sure that their punishment will be swift and sure. As for Arthur Jacobs, I am inclined to feel sorry for him for his record in the government service up to this time had been excellent and I will do all that I can to help him."

Then Waldo Edgar turned to Tully Ross.

"As a result of your work on this case, I am pleased to be able to tell you that you are now a full fledged federal agent."

The chief of the bureau of investigation then faced Bob and he smiled warmly as he spoke.

"To you, Bob, I extend my most sincere congratulations. You were under a great strain, yet you used your head every minute of the time and when the showdown came, you were in there fighting. I don't know when anything has pleased me more than to hand you your commission as a federal agent. You're young, but I predict that as Agent Nine you are going a long ways in the federal service."

In spite of himself, tears welled into Bob's eyes for his heart was overflowing with happiness.

"I'll do my best to make good," he promised. "When do I go on another case?"

Waldo Edgar chuckled. "You'd better rest a day or two from this one. There will be plenty for you later."

He was, indeed, a wise prophet, for in less than 24 hours Bob was to get the call that was to send him out on the famous Jewel Mystery, about which you will learn in "Agent Nine and the Jewel Mystery."

THE END

www.ingramcontent.com/pod-product-compliance
Lightning Source LLC
Chambersburg PA
CBHW050417260626
47156CB00003B/1050